PRAISE FOR ELEANOR TAYLOR BLAND AND HER MARTI MacALISTER NOVELS

DEAD TIME

"A MOST WELCOME ADDITION TO CRIME FICTION."—Sara Paretsky

"BRILLIANT . . . A MAJOR NEW TALENT."
—Nancy Pickard, author of *I.O.U.*

"Bland's herione, Marti MacAlister, is as grounded in reality as her fictional turf."—*Chicago Tribune*

"AUSPICIOUS . . . Bland handles the evolving relationship between Marti and a white male partner unsure of a woman's place in the police world with sensitivity and humor."—*Publishers Weekly*

"A KNOCK-OUT BOOK. It grabbed me from the first page."—Susan Dunlap

SLOW BURN

"Marti MacAlister is attractive and sympathetic—as large as life."—*Los Angeles Times*

"Marti MacAlister is one of the more credible policewomen I have come across . . . and one of the most credible and appealing human beings as well. . . . This a very good book. . . . When you put it down, you'll do so with a feeling of satisfaction, and anticipation of the next."—*Mystery News*

"Marti has stamina . . . in the proliferating world of female crime-solvers."—*Book World*

ELEANOR TAYLOR BLAND, the author of *Dead Time* and *Slow Burn*, lives in Waukegan, Illinois, where she is at work on the fourth Marti MacAlister novel. She is a member of Sisters in Crime and Mystery Writers of America.

G O N E
QUIET

ELEANOR TAYLOR BLAND

A SIGNET BOOK

SIGNET
Published by the Penguin Group
Penguin Books USA Inc., 375 Hudson Street,
New York, New York 10014, U.S.A.
Penguin Books Ltd, 27 Wrights Lane,
London W8 5TZ, England
Penguin Books Australia Ltd, Ringwood,
Victoria, Australia
Penguin Books Canada Ltd, 10 Alcorn Avenue,
Toronto, Ontario, Canada M4V 3B2
Penguin Books (N.Z.) Ltd, 182–190 Wairau Road,
Auckland 10, New Zealand

Penguin Books Ltd, Registered Offices:
Harmondsworth, Middlesex, England

Published by Signet, an imprint of Dutton Signet,
a division of Penguin Books USA Inc. This is an
authorized reprint of a hardcover edition published by St. Martin's Press.
For information address St. Martin's Press, 175 Fifth Avenue,
New York, N.Y. 10010.

First Signet Printing, May, 1995
10 9 8 7 6 5 4 3 2 1

 REGISTERED TRADEMARK—MARCA REGISTRADA

Printed in the United States of America

PUBLISHER'S NOTE
This is a work of fiction. Names, characters, places, and incidents either are
the product of the author's imagination or are used fictitiously, and any
resemblance to actual persons, living or dead, events, or locales is entirely
coincidental.

BOOKS ARE AVAILABLE AT QUANTITY DISCOUNTS WHEN USED TO PROMOTE PROD-
UCTS OR SERVICES. FOR INFORMATION PLEASE WRITE TO PREMIUM MARKETING
DIVISION, PENGUIN BOOKS USA INC., 375 HUDSON STREET, NEW YORK, NEW
YORK 10014.

In appreciation for my continued good health, this book is dedicated to Fabrizio Michelassi, M.D., associate professor of surgery; Juliano Testa, M.D.; Arunus Gasparaitis, M.D.; John Curran, R.T.; Debbie Mhoon, R.N.; Michele Rubin, R.N., M.S.N.; Connie Kelly, R.N., M.S.N.; Jan Cauldwell, R.N., M.S.N.; and the surgical and nursing staff on 4SW and 4SE at the University of Chicago Medical Center, Bernard Mitchell Hospital.

For technical assistance I'd like to acknowledge Sharon Laughlin, Waukegan Historical Society; Rose Mcelyea, Waukegan Regional Airport; Douglas Rhone, Chairman, Department of Pathology, Illinois Masonic Medical Center; John Rorabeck, Lake County Coroners Office; The Red Herrings, and Megan and Kate, Botanical Gardens, Glencoe; and also the Reverend Olen Arrington, Jr., Monica Behnke, Dave Bockrath, Eunice Fikso, Connie Folleth, Dolores Ziolkowski Doyle, Bruce Rasmussen, Greg Schuenemann, Janice Merrell Stuckey, Joe Szpylman, Ruth Ward, Pheobe Waterman, and Bob Zuiker.

Special thanks to the boys in the break room.

P R O L O G U E

When Gladys Hamilton reached the door to her husband's room Saturday morning, she wanted to run away. Anywhere. Away from Henry. Away from today. She took one deep, ragged breath and grasped the doorknob, her knuckles going white as she calmed herself by picturing him dead in his bed. The image soothed her. Twisting the knob, she went in.

Henry's body was stiff beneath the covers. His head was almost off the pillow and his shoulder was leaning slightly to one side. It was so quiet in here without the sound of his snoring . . . and she would never hear him call her name again.

Her knees began to buckle and she leaned against the wall, breathing deeply. He was dead. Imagining his death had always seemed dream-like, but now it was real. She had not wanted him to die so easily or so quickly. She had done the best she could, using what she knew would make him sickly and weak but not knowing how much would kill him. If she could have remembered more of what Grandma told her about working roots, she would have tried that. He should have died years ago.

He was turned toward the window. She stared at him, without looking at his face, until the pain in the small of her back and the ache in her neck and shoulders became more real than the stillness of a body that wasn't breathing anymore. There was no reason to fear the dead, she reminded herself. It was only the living who could hurt you.

She stepped over the shirt Henry had dropped on the floor, kicked his thick gray socks to one side, and walked around his shoes, heavy brogans caked with mud. He'd been out in the garden yesterday, making sure the neighbors' boy had pulled up all the dead plants, deciding how he wanted the vegetables rotated in the spring, and telling her where to put the lime in because they'd had slugs this year. She had listened, certain that by spring she would be making the decisions and the yard would be seeded for grass.

When she got close to his bed and leaned over to get a look at his face, Henry's eyes were open in a wide-eyed stare. She liked the way he looked, as if he'd been scared at the end. A trickle of spittle had oozed down one side of his mouth and dried there.

For a moment she remembered him young, his face looking like it was struck from bronze. He had a serious, unsmiling face, cleft chin and high cheekbones, thin lips. She'd thought him handsome then. She had tried to get him to smile, to laugh. She had thought for a long time that he spoke to her so seldom because he regretted marrying her. She was darker than he was, not pretty like that high yellow woman he was courting when they met. Now she wondered why it had taken so many years of blaming herself before she saw that his own perversity kept him the way he was.

She thought of what Henry had done with her hats yesterday and kicked at his shoes. He had become even more ornery in his old age, and meaner. It was good that he was gone. She took his pipes off of the nightstand, threw them and the ashtray into the wastebasket, tossed in the humidor and the leather pouch half-filled with tobacco. Now she would be rid of the sight and the smell of him.

Leaving the room, she walked down the hall, trailing her fingers along the edge of the narrow shelf he had put up along its length. The shelf was crowded with every ashtray he'd ever been able to get his hands on that advertised something: products, cities, states, hotels, and restaurants. More than half of them were stolen, even though he was a deacon of the church.

For close to thirty-five years she had listened to him criticize and complain. For thirty-five years she had smelled that stinking old pipe. It seemed as if she'd spent all of her life in this house with him. She shivered, hugging herself for a moment. Now she would have this place to herself. Do as she pleased.

She went into her own smaller, neater room. Everything was in its place and smelled of lavender sachet, just as her mother's bedroom had. She went to the closet, decided to wear her green dress. It was soft and dark, made of lamb's wool and angora. Not something she could afford. Her daughter Denise had given it to her.

She smoothed down a cotton slip over her snuggies and added two half-slips. She was always cold unless she wore plenty of clothes. Even when she was younger, Henry had called her an old woman because of all the underwear, but she would never wear slacks unless she was working in the yard. Henry wouldn't allow the thermostat to be set higher than sixty-eight, so this was the only way she could keep warm.

As she slipped on crepe-soled shoes she wondered if she'd have time to go to the store today and buy herself shoes with just a little heel to them. Shoes and hats had been her only vanities when she met Henry. Now she was tired of wearing all this rubber just because he didn't want marks on the parquet floors in the living room and dining room. No use telling him these kind of shoes drew on her feet and made them swell when she had to wear them all day.

She went back to his room and looked at him. She took a credit card out of his wallet. It was issued in both their names, but he had never allowed her to use it. Starting today she could do as she pleased. She could buy herself a new hat, too. He'd gotten angry Wednesday when she'd asked for one, called her a pride-filled strumpet. Thursday he had taken all of them but one old black felt that she'd had for years and put them out with the garbage.

He had had that pleased look on his face all day, but she wouldn't give him the satisfaction of asking why. Then, after dinner, he had told her what he had done. "And if Dolly or Denise replaces nar one of them, I'll throw that away, too. Vanity will not be allowed to thrive in my house." That was the first thing she was going to do with whatever was left over from the insurance. Buy some new hats. She took such pleasure in shopping for herself, and Henry wouldn't be here to deny her.

By the time she was dressed, Gladys was humming. It was Saturday. She always went to her sister Dolly's house Saturday morning, stayed overnight, and met Henry at church for Sunday morning service. No need to do anything different today. There would be time enough to take care of Henry tomorrow. Time enough for all of that bother when she got back from church.

She closed the door to his room. If there was any odor after one day it wouldn't go any farther than that. She turned the thermostat as low as it would go. And she'd better let Henry's cat stay outside, put some food by the back door. She loved that old man, Bootsie did. Poor old cat. As old as she was, close to twelve, Henry had put her out last night and forgotten to let her back in. At least with the cat, she wouldn't be all alone now.

Maybe she ought to call Denise this evening, have her look in on him. It probably wouldn't bother Denise if she found him dead. He wasn't her real daddy, after all. Gladys had asked Denise to check on him a couple of other Saturdays when he wouldn't answer her nine-o'clock phone call. He would have fussed at her all week if she didn't call him from her sister's house. Denise hadn't liked coming over. But this would be the last time.

C H A P T E R

1

There were so many cars on Chestnut Street that Marti had to park a block away on a side street and walk to the house where the death had been reported. If she were still in Chicago she would have double-parked in front of the house, but if she did that here in Lincoln Prairie, just sixty miles north of the big city, some public-spirited citizen would complain to everyone from his alderman to the chief of police.

As she got out of the car, she debated whether to take her camera. The call seemed routine. Dispatch said the victim was elderly. He had died at home alone, and it looked like natural causes, which would mean a routine death investigation. Better to take the camera, she decided, than wish that she had later if the coroner ruled otherwise.

She was in one of two subdivisions referred to

as the Preserves because of their proximity to a forest preserve. The streets were laid out in a grid, and the locals could tell one subdivision from the other by the street names.

In this section the streets were named for trees. The two- and three-bedroom bungalows were almost identical, varying only in the color of the aluminum siding, whether there was a garage, and the location of the door to the kitchen, side or rear.

In the next section, everyone lived in a ranch or trilevel and the streets were named for poets. Her first arrest here, three days after she joined the force, had been a domestic homicide on Shakespeare Road. The woman had walked into the family room, shot her husband while he was working his way through enough alcohol to get primed for her weekly beating, and called the police.

Marti pushed a tricycle out of her way and into a yard. She could hear children arguing inside one of the houses, until a man yelled, "Shut up!" The living room light went out but the television stayed on.

It was ten o'clock. The sky was so dark and clear that she could see the blinking lights of an airplane as it navigated a path beneath the stars. A three-quarter moon hung low enough to glimpse between tree branches with the last leaves of autumn still clinging, brown and crisp.

It was November, cold enough for the lined raincoat that she was wearing over the slack suit she'd put on when she got the call.

Again she wondered about the cars, parked bumper to bumper the length of the block. Each house had a driveway, some with large, older model vehicles or pickup trucks, some with Hondas or Escorts or Blazers. There was no music or other signs of a party. She began checking mailboxes. The Hamilton house was the third in from the corner, with an addition built on the back, as quiet as the others but packed with people.

"What the hell?" Marti asked Mary Jane Jensen, the uniform who opened the door. "Who let all these people in here?"

The tall, slender, dark-haired officer stepped outside, leaving the door ajar. She gave Marti a blue-eyed stare. "It was like this when we got here. I've never seen anything like it. You'll have to explain it to me."

Marti caught the implication. She was black, like the Hamiltons and most of the people inside. She wasn't offended—she didn't think Jensen had much social contact with African Americans.

"I have never seen anything like this," Jensen repeated, shaking her head. "His stepdaughter came over to check on him. She found him dead and called us. Then she called her minister so he could break it to her mother, who was at choir practice. Whoever took the message must have told everyone at church, and from the looks of it they all came over here. No consideration for the family at all."

"They've come to do whatever they can to help," Marti explained. "We all come together when someone dies. I'm surprised they're so quiet."

"They weren't when we got here," Jensen said. "Most of the women were crying. It wasn't easy getting them to settle down."

"Well, food's next," Marti said. "Nickel bet we've only got half the church membership here now, and the other half is home cooking something to tide the family over until after the funeral."

"There could be a big problem if this isn't natural causes. We tried, but . . ." Jensen shrugged. "By the time my partner and I got here they were all over the place, in the bedroom, touching that poor man, kissing him." She shuddered. "People were leaving as we arrived. I don't think they actually moved him, but there's something about the position of the body. We got everyone out except the daughter. I thought we'd have a riot on our hands if we made her leave. They insisted someone in the family had to stay with him. We did all we could."

Marti was impressed that the two of them had

managed to clear the bedroom. She knew more than a few church sisters who would have refused to budge until a higher authority, like the pastor or God, told them that they had to leave.

"Jessenovik here?" she asked. Vik was her partner. She hadn't spotted his car.

"Not yet. Nobody's shown up from the coroner's office, either. Dispatch said the coroner's out of town."

Marti hoped that whoever was filling in for the coroner, Janet Petrosky, would bring her favorite pathologist, Dr. Cyprian, along.

"Where's the deceased?"

"The body's in a back bedroom."

Marti pushed open the front door and stepped into the living room. She recognized everyone there, about thirty people, as about one-third of the Mount Gethsemane Baptist Church adult choir. Marti belonged to Greater Faith Baptist. Each church visited the other twice a year, so Marti assumed that just about everyone present recognized her, too. Rehearsals were not a casual affair. About the only difference between dressing for them or for Sunday services was whether or not you wore a hat. At least a dozen different kinds of perfume competed for top scent, creating an odor that made her think of thousands of flowers, crushed and dying.

At five-ten and 160 pounds, Marti never had a problem shouldering her way through a crowd.

She did so now without speaking. One of the younger members stopped crying long enough to whisper, "What's she doing here?"

Marti made her way past everyone, nodding silently. It was the first time she'd been assigned to a case that involved anyone she knew socially, but it was unlikely to be the last. The population in Lincoln Prairie was only ninety thousand. It was a small town compared to Chicago, where she'd been on the force for ten years. Thinking about it, she was surprised this hadn't happened sooner.

The serious mourners were in the kitchen. Five women stood in a tight circle holding on to each other. The one with the walker had to be at least seventy-five, Marti thought, and another was close to her own age, almost forty.

"Old Henry done slipped away from us and gone home."

"A good man, sister. Such a good man."

"Sure gonna miss him."

"Won't see the likes of him pass this way again."

"Be with Jesus now. Be with the Lord."

She had heard these words spoken since childhood, as if the mourners were repeating phrases from an old beloved spiritual. Marti thought of the numbness she had felt when she buried her husband two and a half years ago. These were the words she remembered.

Three men were huddled in the corner, clasping hands. Deacon Gilmore prayed aloud. "We know that in your time, Lord, you called him home. Keep him now, Lord, and in your kindness and mercy, bless those of us who mourn."

There was a chorus of amens.

Marti went over to the men and spoke to Mr. Franklin, the head deacon, a frail, bespectacled elderly man.

"Where's Mrs. Hamilton?"

"Pastor hasn't brought her home yet. I expect she'll be here soon. I'm so glad they sent you, Sister MacAlister. It's always nice to see one of our own."

"I suppose everyone's viewed the body?"

The old man chuckled. "Sounding just like a police officer now, ain't you. Yes ma'am, you know they did. You want to see him too you just go right that way." He pointed toward a doorway, then shook his head. "Henry was ten years younger than me and just up and died." He snapped his fingers. "We got to be watchful, know not the day nor the hour. I just saw Henry Wednesday night at the deacons' meeting." His eyes filled. "Now he's gone quiet into the night to be with the Lord."

Marti went where he pointed, to a hall that led to another door. A uniform stepped aside to let her into the bedroom. Marti recognized him as a rookie. "You and your partner did a good

19

job clearing the room and keeping everyone out," she told him.

He looked pleased.

A woman was sitting upright in a thickly upholstered recliner. The only light came from a small bedside lamp. The woman's face was in shadows. Marti was surprised to recognize Denise Stevens.

Marti went to her. "Denise, are you okay?"

Denise nodded.

"Is there anything I can do?"

She shook her head. "There's not much anyone can do now."

Marti knew Denise as a rather stern juvenile probation officer who was given the hard-core offenders because she had a lot more success with them than anyone else. She could recall a few comments about Denise being single and childless, but never any gossip.

Denise was a tall, large-boned woman, like Marti, but not comfortable with her size, as Marti was. Every time Marti saw her she was wearing severely tailored suits in dark or neutral colors, never a ruffle or bow, never the red or blue or yellow accents that Marti loved. Denise nearly always wore an elaborate hat that drew attention to her face, which was darker than Marti's, and away from her hips, which were broader. Tonight there was no hat. Without one, dark hair framed her face in short, feathery curls.

Denise was pretty in a way unique to dark-skinned women, an attractiveness that would not diminish with age. Her face was as smooth as fine-grained mahogany, her almond-shaped eyes dark and expressive. Denise wasn't crying, hadn't been crying. She was looking at the body with something that seemed close to dislike. An instinct deeper than curiosity made Marti wonder why.

"Sorry to have to intrude, but I need to ask you a few questions." It felt awkward to be formal with someone she knew professionally, but she thought it was more appropriate than being too familiar.

"Sure, MacAlister. I know you have to investigate and there has to be an autopsy because he died here alone. And I've called Ezra Whittaker, the funeral director. My youngest sister is married to him. What happens now?"

"We have to wait for the coroner and the MD. Do you check on your stepfather often?"

"No, just when he gets ornery and won't answer mother's calls." Denise looked at the dead man, her eyes bright, but not with tears.

"My mother goes to her sister's every Saturday morning. My Aunt Dolly's a widow. Mother stays there overnight and they go to church together Sunday morning and meet my stepfather there."

21

"Was he okay when she left today?"

"I assume so."

"Has he been ill?"

"For about a year and a half. They don't tell me much, but I assume he had heart trouble because mother mentioned his 'condition,' and cancer, which mother referred to as 'that.' I don't know how bad it was or what kind of treatment he was getting. We took him to the hospital several times . . . and the way he was losing weight . . ." Her voice trailed off, almost as if she'd lost interest in talking about him. Marti noticed that she kept clenching and unclenching her hands.

"Was he taking medication?"

"He drank herb tea. Believed in stuff like ginseng, garlic, and castor oil. Probably ate oysters, too. I can't say if he was treating himself or taking something prescribed or just trying to ignore whatever was wrong. He was good at that, ignoring things."

"Who's the family doctor?"

"I don't know about him, VA hospital, maybe. Mother went to Dr. Larson over on Webster. I can check the medicine cabinet for you, see if anyone prescribed anything."

"Is it okay if I have a uniform take care of that?"

"Sure."

Marti gave instructions to the uniform. "Also," she told him, "don't go around asking anyone

22

who they are, but make sure there's a list of everyone present and everyone who stopped in for a few minutes."

The rookie looked at her, confused.

"There's an elderly man in the kitchen, Mr. Franklin. He'll help you. Tell him I'd like to know. And ask him if there's anyone he thinks should be here who isn't."

She went back to Denise, notebook open. "I need to know his full name."

"Henry Isaiah Hamilton."

"Age?"

"He turned seventy in September."

"When is the last time you saw him alive?"

"Last Sunday. This is the first time I've been over here since."

Technically, since the cause of death appeared to be illness or natural causes, Marti could not do anything invasive, even open a drawer, without permission. Out of habit, her request was nonspecific. "I'd like to look around. Is that okay?"

"Sure."

"Do you want to stay here?"

"I can't leave. There'd be talk about it for a month," Denise said, her voice quiet, without inflection. "But do whatever you have to. I'll keep out of your way." She gripped one hand with the other as she sat stiffly in the chair, which looked comfortable enough to fall asleep in.

Marti put on a pair of latex gloves. She didn't want to add her fingerprints to the dozens of others that probably could be found here. She took out her camera and circled the full-size bed. The pillow and blankets on the side nearest the wall looked undisturbed. Not much to do until the coroner arrived. No reason to call in the evidence techs.

Mr. Hamilton had been dead long enough for rigor mortis to set in, approximately twelve hours, depending on such factors as room temperature. The room was cool.

"Were the windows closed when you came in here?" Marti asked Denise.

"They're always closed. He didn't like fresh air. Mother opens hers every day, year-round."

"My mother does the same thing," Marti said. "She still insists that fresh air kills germs." She went to the door and told the rookie to check the thermostat.

"It was off when we got here. Since then, someone's turned it on," he said.

Marti turned to Denise. "Do you know if they always keep the house this cool?"

"It's always cold in here in the winter. Momma wears sweaters and kneesocks around the house. He keeps the thermostat at sixty-eight."

It felt closer to fifty now.

Marti moved closer to the body. The smell wasn't bad. Urine, but only close up. The angle of the head on the pillow seemed unusual. As far as she could tell the body hadn't been moved after death; no signs that the rigor had been broken, no lividity to suggest that the body had been in a different position when the blood pooled.

The old man was tall, at least six feet. His hair was gray, thin on top, and clipped short. She could see his scalp. There was a bristle of gray stubble on his face. His tan complexion was pallid, as if he had been in poor health for a while, and had a waxy, death-mask look. His cheeks were sunken, as if he had recently lost weight. Marti tried to imagine what he might have looked like as a younger or healthier man. There were no photographs in the room to help her.

She noticed another odor, leaned closer, and sniffed. Tobacco, with a particular scent, hickory maybe. He had smoked a pipe. She glanced at the wastebasket, then took a closer look. All of his smoking things had been dumped in there. Odd. She snapped a picture.

Marti tried not to be too intrusive, although Denise did not appear to be at all upset. Maybe Denise was in shock. Marti wished she'd had more contact with her, professional or social. Maybe this was just her normal way of dealing with grief. Somehow, though, she didn't believe that.

Marti used up the twenty-four-exposure roll of black-and-whites and switched to color film. The angle of the head continued to bother her. She took pictures of the pillow indentation, which could have been caused by the head as it lay in a more natural position. She looked closely at the head, picturing it as it could have been on the indentation, faceup. Then she stood away from the bed, moving in a circular direction, taking pictures of the body in relationship to the rest of the room.

"Are you always this thorough?" Denise asked.

"Always," Marti said.

"Even when it's natural causes?"

Marti turned to look at Denise and saw her partner Vik in the doorway.

C H A P T E R
2

Vik's wiry gray eyebrows bunched in a scowl. Tomorrow was supposed to be their first day off in almost three weeks, but this would probably cancel it. He looked more than a little ticked off. At forty-nine, Vik was senior man on a 129-person force with an average age of thirty-two. He was used to the long hours, but tired tonight, just as Marti was.

Marti dropped the two rolls of film she had shot into her pocket as she looked up at him. He wasn't much taller than she was, and he stayed thin no matter how much he ate, but tonight his loosely belted trench coat created an illusion of bulk. He had said he was going to the barbershop when they left the precinct this evening, but he still needed a haircut. His salt-and-pepper hair always sprang back to its usual disarray almost as soon as he combed it, and now it hung almost to his collar as well. That, along with the pouches under his eyes and his nose, broken years ago, gave an impression of suppressed ferocity that could be intimidating to people who didn't know him.

Vik appraised the situation, giving the body a brooding stare that Marti had seen before. He usually followed it with a remark like, "When people just up and die they should do it when it's convenient for the rest of us." Reports of deaths due to natural causes never seemed to come between nine and five on weekdays. He was more sympathetic when it was a homicide. Marti remembered him saying once, on a murder scene at three in the morning, "Poor Joey. He might have been a pain-in-the-ass two-bit thief since he was nine, but a knife in the throat is a hell of a way to go."

Marti arranged her camera and lenses in their case. When she looked up, Vik was glaring at the back of the recliner. When Denise turned toward him he seemed as surprised as Marti had been to see their favorite juvenile probation officer sitting there.

"Oh, uh, Miss Stevens," he said, his voice gruff. "Sorry about your father."

"Stepfather," Denise corrected, and resumed her vigil.

Vik turned to Marti and made jabbing motions in the direction of the kitchen and living room, disgruntled at the crowd that had congregated. "Anyone else been in here?"

Marti stifled a grin. "About half the adult choir of Mount Gethsemane Baptist Church. Maybe forty, fifty people."

Vik took in every surface of the room, cataloging the potential damage. Dozens of smudged prints, lost chain of evidence, obliterated clues, total devastation if this turned out to be the scene of a crime. His Adam's apple bobbed as he swallowed back at least half a dozen expletives and his favorite Polish death threats. He cleared his throat, probably to keep from choking.

When he scowled at Marti, she shrugged in response. The crowd had arrived before she did. It wasn't her fault that everyone had tramped through here. They were friends of the family.

Vik gave her an impatient jerk of his thumb, as if they should order Denise to leave. Marti raised her eyebrows. As far as she knew there hadn't been a crime. There was no reason why the dead man's stepdaughter shouldn't be in the room with his body.

Vik looked from Denise to the corpse and made a sniffing motion with his nose. He didn't like the position of Hamilton's head either. Marti gave him a small nod.

It was a cozy room with maple furniture and paneling, moss green carpet, drapes, and comforter. The room made Marti think of a burrow hollowed out of a tree trunk. A double bed, one side unslept in. Nothing in sight that belonged to a woman. Seating for one. And isolated from the rest of the house.

A place for everything and everything in its place, Marti thought. His slippers were aligned by the side of the bed, and a heavy velour bathrobe was folded at the foot. Magazines were stacked in a pile on the table beside the chair, this month's *Ebony* on top, a radio beside them. No television or stereo equipment. The bureau was just as tidy. Cologne and deodorant containers were arranged by size. A tray with pairs of cufflinks and two watches, one silver, one gold, side by side.

The nightstand was noticeably bare. Two small clocks, one a wind-up, the ticking just audible, and one electric. The pipes and tobacco and ashtray that should have been there had been thrown away . . . possibly by someone who knew they wouldn't be needed again. Perhaps he had decided to quit smoking.

When Vik took a step into the room, Marti nodded toward the wastebasket so he would amble over and glance at the contents. Vik acknowledged this with one raised eyebrow then made a small gesture toward the clothing on the floor.

Blue-and-white-striped boxer shorts were partially covered by a blue-plaid flannel shirt. Mud had dried on the boots and fallen off in black clumps. Mr. Hamilton might have liked to have everything in order, but someone had to pick up after him. The same person who had filled the wastebasket? Marti was looking forward to meeting the widow.

A sudden loud burst of conversation from elsewhere in the house subsided quickly, as if someone had turned off the sound. A few minutes later Officer Jensen came to the door with Mrs. Hamilton. She was a tiny woman with skin the color of a copper penny and a scattering of freckles across high cheekbones. Naturally straight black hair with wide silver streaks was coiled in a cornrowed braid around her head. Indian ancestry, Marti decided.

There was no physical resemblance between mother and daughter, but no questioning the relationship, either. Denise got up at once, put her arm about her mother's shoulders, and shielded her from seeing the body.

Mother spoke to daughter in a voice just above a whisper. Marti recognized the dialect as Gullah, spoken on the Sea Islands along the coast of South Carolina. It had been a long time since she'd listened, both puzzled and fascinated, to a neighbor woman talking that way.

Gladys became agitated as she said something about hats. Denise tried to shush her, and

Gladys calmed down. Marti made out the word "teefin'," which was thieving, or stealing, but she was unable to decipher much of what Gladys was saying. She concentrated on the cadence and picked up what she thought was, "The old man done gone and left us, chile." Then, "We be well rid of that old fool."

Denise spoke calmly. "You're all right, m'dear?"

Marti had often called her own mother that.

Gladys nodded and the two women turned to Marti, both avoiding any glimpse of the body. The old woman's pointy jaw jutted, and her dark eyes showed no sign of weeping. Marti thought of the clothing discarded on the floor and didn't feel judgmental.

"Mrs. Hamilton, we're here because this happened at home."

"I understand." All traces of the Gullah were gone. There was strength in her voice, and Marti saw a lot of Denise in that. If she ignored physical appearances, the women seemed very much alike.

"I need to ask you a few questions." Marti knew she should at least suggest going into another room, but she wanted them here to see how they reacted to being near the body.

Instead of answering, Mrs. Hamilton gripped Denise's arm and turned toward the bed. For a moment her face seemed filled with anger, then little creases appeared until she seemed sad. Shaking her head, she said, "Poor Henry."

As her mother spoke, Denise moved away from her so slightly that the shift was almost imperceptible. Marti saw a tightness at the corners of her mouth that went away as her mother leaned against her again. The top of Mrs. Hamilton's head just reached Denise's shoulder. For a moment Marti thought Denise wanted to push her mother away. Instead, Denise said, "Here, sit down."

Marti considered the questions she wanted to ask, and decided to begin with how Mrs. Hamilton had spent the day. Instead of relaxing, the woman remained tense but gave quick, detailed answers, pointing out that the shoes she was wearing had been purchased just this afternoon, and were the most comfortable she'd owned in years. Then she described her new hat.

After ten minutes of listening to extended detours around the fact that a man was lying dead in his bed, Marti asked, "How was your husband the last time you saw him?"

Without hesitation, Mrs. Hamilton said, "Asleep."

"Was that this morning or last night?"

"Evening."

"You didn't come in here this morning?"

Denise squeezed her mother's arm.

"I looked in," Gladys said. "He was sleeping."

"What's the last thing he ate, that you know of?"

"Cocoa. And four chocolate mint cookies."

"What time was that?"

"Nine o'clock."

"Last night, ma'am?"

"Of course. You could set your watch by it."

Denise interrupted. "It's been a long evening, and it's not over yet."

"I know," Marti agreed. "And I'm sorry I have to bother you with this."

An anxious, middle-aged man whom Marti recognized as the coroner's assistant came into the room.

"Where's Janet?" Marti asked.

"Oregon. Her daughter had a little girl on Thursday." He extended his hand. "Rick Fields."

Marti's handshake was less than enthusiastic. She had never worked with Fields and had come to rely on Janet's quiet competence. When the doctor came in, a young woman she didn't know, Marti looked at Vik. He shrugged.

"Carrie Nichols," the doctor said. She was as tall as Marti, but thinner and wore a denim skirt and jacket. She didn't look old enough to be out of medical school for more than a couple of years.

Rick Fields spoke to the widow.

"Now Mrs. Hamilton, the doctor will just be a little while. Perhaps there's someplace where we can talk. Let's decide how I can be of assistance."

With that, he shepherded Mrs. Hamilton out of the room. Denise followed closely behind. Vik waited until the women left, took another look into the wastebasket, then followed Marti into the hall. Neither of them had ever worked with this doctor before. Marti hoped she was as thorough as Dr. Cyprian.

In the hall, Vik covered his mouth with his hand and whispered, "Why couldn't he wait until tomorrow morning to die? The choir would've been in church. Tomorrow afternoon would have been even better, then I could have gotten a decent night's sleep and I'd be able to go to church, too. Damned inconsiderate."

He scuffed his foot on the carpet as if he wished he could kick something. "This better be natural causes. We won't have any evidence to support anything else. I don't suppose anybody could resist the urge to touch his forehead or kiss his cheek when they paraded through there. That's probably why his head is that way. Not that we'll ever know for sure. It's a wonder anyone even bothered to call us," he fumed. "Not much we can do now that they've swarmed all over the place. We could just leave, all the good it's doing us to hang around."

"Could," Marti agreed.

"Oh, come on, Marti. Don't tell me you've got some kind of hunch."

"I just wonder who threw the pipes and tobacco away. And when. Too bad Denise Stevens is involved. She's a damned good probation officer. Otherwise, I don't know her that well."

Vik frowned. "I don't think anyone does. She didn't even show up for Midget's retirement, and the guy was a dispatcher for thirty-six years. The mayor, city council, my wife, and retirees I thought were dead came to that party."

Marti looked at the closed door to Hamilton's room. There were no photographs in there and none in the living room either, not even of Denise's high school graduation. Almost everyone Marti knew displayed those.

"The position of the head bothers me," Vik said. "Maybe he had a seizure of some kind."

"Could have. Apparently he had heart trouble and cancer."

They heard more commotion at the front of the house and a woman burst into the hallway, rushing toward them.

"Where is he?" the woman demanded, swaying as she stopped in front of Marti and steadying herself by bracing an arm on the wall. She had an auburn ponytail pinned to black hair, and she was wrapped in what looked like fake fur. "Who are you? And just what in the hell are you doing here?" Her breath smelled like she'd just chuga-lugged a fifth of scotch.

"I'm Detective MacAlister."

The woman swayed forward. "Cops? Who killed him? Who went and killed the old bastard?"

When the woman attempted to enter the bedroom, Marti said, "You can see him, but I'd appreciate it if you'd wait a few minutes. The doctor's in there."

"What? He ain't dead yet? Just like that old son of a—"

The woman belched, then covered her mouth. She was as tall as Denise, with the same dark skin and oval eyes.

"May I ask your name?" Marti said, aware of her soft spot for drunks.

"Where's my mother?" the woman demanded. "I wanna see my mother. Right now. Where have you taken her? What have you done to my mother?"

"You're Mrs. Hamilton's daughter?"

"That's right. What's it to you? Belle, name's Belle, Belle Stevens." Turning with a lurch that made her bump into the wall, Belle yelled, "Denise! Where the hell are you? Denise! They done took Momma to jail for doin' the old bastard in. Denise, where are you?"

Turning to Vik, Belle put her finger to her mouth. "Shhh. Denise's good people. Too damned good, if you ask me. Know what I mean?" She rocked back on her heels, squinting up at Vik. "You ain't a cop too?"

Vik nodded.

"Damn. And you looked like you might be halfway decent."

With that she turned and headed toward the kitchen. Marti nodded to Vik and they followed.

C H A P T E R
3

The nutmeg-and-cinnamon aroma of hot peach cobbler greeted Marti as she followed Belle into the kitchen. Three boxes of fast-food chicken were on the table, and one side of the sink was filled with ice and cans of pop.

Belle kicked off her shoes and threw her coat on a chair. She was wearing a chartreuse satin dress with gold sequins scattered across the low-cut bodice. The hem stopped mid-thigh. She gave Deacon Gilmore a defiant toss of her head, then turned to the women. "Mother Franklin! How you been?" She put her arms around the frailest of the five women, and bent to kiss her forehead.

"Why I'm just fine, child," Mrs. Franklin said. "It's so good to see you again. Too bad something like this has brought us together."

"Past time that old fool died." Belle's voice was husky.

"Both of us know you cared more than that."

"Don't know no such a thing," Belle replied, but she blinked back tears as she hugged Mother Franklin again and backed away from her, steadier on her feet without her shoes. "Take care of yourself now, promise."

Marti walked behind Belle as she headed for the living room and heard her mutter, "Now I gotta be bothered with these stuck-up, seditty, loose-lipped witches. That old bastard coulda picked a better time to die. I don't hardly feel like bein' bothered with none of this tonight."

Everyone in the living room was close to Belle's age, which Marti guessed was about thirty-five. Nobody spoke when Belle walked in.

"Nice to see y'all again too," Belle said. She squared her shoulders and sashayed past them with a rhythmic sway of her hips.

Mrs. Hamilton was in a bedroom about half the size of her husband's. She was sitting on a mahogany four-poster that looked antique. Denise was sitting beside her. The acting coroner had left.

Belle hesitated in the doorway and put her hand where her dress didn't quite cover her breasts. "Momma, I'm sorry. I wouldn't have come here if I knew all these people . . ."

Denise got up and touched Belle's face, pushing back a strand of black hair in a maternal, carressing gesture. Then Denise put her arm about Belle's waist, hugging her. "It's all right, baby. Don't you worry none about any of them."

Belle let Denise lead her over to the bed. She sat as far from her mother as possible and began to sniffle. "I'm so sorry to come here like this, Momma."

Gladys's chin jutted out. Marti guessed that she was angry or embarrassed.

Marti took a quick look about the room, which seemed more frugal than Mr. Hamilton's. The threadbare rug didn't quite cover the floor, unlike the plush wall-to-wall carpet in his room. The curtains were limp organdy priscillas with a few small holes showing against the drawn shades. A white chenille bedspread was folded back and the sheets showed signs of mending. Marti caught a whiff of lavender and thought of her own mother's room.

There was a twelve-by-fifteen-inch print of *Christ Knocking at the Door* over the bed, and a smaller portrait of Jesus in profile above the cluttered bureau. Clothes had been tossed on a chair. A Bible, bound in cracked black leather with most of the gilt rubbed off the edges, was on the nightstand.

Denise rubbed her eyes and yawned, then spoke to Marti. "I've got to get someone to start moving these people out. Is there anything you need me to do?"

"Keep the door to his room locked until after the post mortem."

"Sure," Denise said, leaning against the wall, arms folded. "They've all been in there at least once anyway. I suppose the food's started coming."

"Peach cobbler smelled good."

"Probably Sister Russell's. Lots of cinnamon and nutmeg. I bet she fixed it for her godchild's wedding tomorrow."

"You look tired," Marti said.

"Not as tired as I'm going to be. My youngest sister hasn't got here. Her husband might not have told her yet. Terri's one of those women who looks terminally ill when she's pregnant. And it seems like she's been carrying this one at least nineteen months."

As they walked toward the living room, Marti could hear a low weeping, almost a keening sound.

"Oh, shit," Denise said. "Terri's here."

A space had been cleared around the sofa. Terri was as petite as her mother, with the same pointy chin and nose, exaggerated by the hollows in her pale face. Her stomach, huge with child, seemed an insupportable burden for someone so tiny. "My daddy," she whimpered. "My daddy."

Although Terri looked just like her mother, she seemed to lack the older woman's vitality.

Marti heard Denise suck in her breath and

saw the tightness at the corners of her mouth. She waited for Denise to go to Terri just as she had gone to Belle, but she did not. Instead, one of the younger women put her arm around Terri's shoulder and began to rock her.

"Wrong thing to do," Denise said.

"My daddy," Terri sobbed. "Daddy. My God, it's my daddy." The decibels increased as the woman rocked her until Terri was screaming, "Daddy! Daddy! Let me see him! Where is he?"

Denise crossed the room and motioned the other woman away. "Terri! Stop this. It's not good for you."

Terri shut up abruptly, as if Denise had slapped her. "You didn't love him," Terri accused. "You're glad he's dead."

"You've got to take care of yourself, Terri." Denise spoke sternly, as if to a child. She reached down to help her sister stand up. "You come along with me and lie down in Momma's room."

An older, stoop-shouldered man stood near the door, watching. With a start, Marti realized he was Ezra Whittaker, Terri's husband.

C H A P T E R

4

A few hours later, after everyone else had left, Denise piled pieces of chicken on a plate and took a large container of potato salad to the kitchen table. She stood by the window for a few minutes, gauging the darkness outside as she leaned against the glass, feeling the coldness on her forehead. Had anyone seen her come here last night? Looking out, she could see only what lay within the radius of the light from the window, a distance of not more than ten feet. She could see the points and angles of the tree branches, and the outlines of the houses on the next block, but everything else was in shadows.

Denise crossed the room to the light switch. When she turned off the light the kitchen wasn't totally dark, and her eyes adjusted right away. She returned to the window. Now there was a light on in the kitchen across from her, creating a yellow rectangle like a window in a child's drawing, but without increasing the visibility outside. There hadn't been any lights on when she came here last night. Was anyone watching?

She sat down. By the time she had eaten four pieces of chicken and most of the potato salad, the light in the other house had gone out. Anyone looking out that window now would see very little.

She should never have come here last night. Damn him for getting rid of all Momma's hats. It was petty and cruel and it infuriated her. She had waited until she knew they would both be sleeping soundly, let herself in, and tiptoed in stocking feet down the hall to his room, looking for Bootsie. That cat was the only thing he loved, besides Terri. Denise had intended to take Bootsie away for a while, although that sounded silly now. She wanted him to know how Momma felt when something that important to her was taken away. She wanted him to wake up without that cat, worry and wonder what had happened to her. But he wouldn't wake up ever again, and she never did find the cat.

Momma must have left this morning without knowing he was dead. Momma. Did she want to be free, or had she become so accustomed to living with him all these years that she no longer knew how to live without him?

Denise ate another piece of chicken, then a

bowl of cobbler. She had wanted him dead for so long, thought about so many ways to kill him, and now he was gone. She tried to delay the sudden rush of guilt, consoling herself with sugar-and-nutmeg-saturated peaches when she could not.

C H A P T E R

5

An hour after the autopsy the following morning, Marti and Vik had a brief conference with Rick Fields and the doctor, Carrie Nichols. Fields's office was that of a man who liked chaos. He looked like such a neat and organized man that Marti was taken aback by the disarray. Papers, some of them coffee-stained, were piled on a table. Journals were stacked on the floor. The bookcase was crammed with books and more papers, with oversize volumes stacked precariously on the top shelf. Marti had to remove folders from a chair in order to sit down. Vik gave the room a look of disgust and stayed near the door.

"I wasn't expecting you two to attend," Fields said.

"His stepdaughter's a member of the department," Vik said, as if that was explanation enough.

"And you didn't give us a cause of death," Marti added.

Dr. Nichols glanced at the door. "You'll have my written report sometime tomorrow."

"How are you calling it?" Vik asked. He was being polite. Even if Nichols hadn't found a feather lodged in Hamilton's throat, they both knew what the hemorrhages in the mucous membranes of his mouth and the pinpoint hemorrhages in his eyes, heart, lungs, and other organs meant. Bruising under the skin indicated that someone had applied pressure to his shoulders.

"Asphyxia," the doctor confirmed. "Someone smothered him."

"What about the hemorrhaging and ulceration in his digestive tract?" Marti asked.

"We ran a Reinsch test for you. It screens for heavy-metal poisons, and there were none present. Nobody's been sneaking him any arsenic. That's all we can do at this facility."

Nichols hadn't wanted to order the test. Marti wasn't sure if the request had irritated her because they were smart enough to ask for it or if she was still inexperienced enough to feel that they were questioning her competence.

"And we have his pillows. The person who handles that is in Wisconsin. He'll examine them tomorrow. We'll also check his medical records, but whatever caused the gastric symptoms is not the cause of death."

"That doesn't mean it's not important," Marti said. "Were there any indications of an underlying disease that could have caused it?"

"None that I observed."

If Janet Petrosky were here she would expand on what they had observed during the autopsy, Marti thought.

"Could it be the result of an allergy that Hamilton wasn't aware of?" Marti persisted.

"Can't say."

"Could someone have deliberately caused it?"

"That's speculation," Rick Fields said.

Frustrated, Marti swore under her breath. "Is it possible that the intestinal inflammation was caused by something he was eating?"

"Yes."

"Could it have been something he ingested once?"

The doctor shook her head.

"Would it have had to be recent?"

"There were no indications of healing."

Dr. Nichols moved toward the door. Vik blocked her path. "His stepdaughter thought he had heart trouble and cancer."

Dr. Nichols shook her head. "He was in remarkably good condition for a man his age. No cardiac problems, and the two abdominal tumors were located in fatty tissue. The odds on malignancy are minimal."

Vik stepped aside.

"You'll let us know as soon as you find out anything else?" Marti said.

Nichols bumped into a pile of journals, scattering several on the floor. She looked at them as if it wasn't worth the effort to pick them up.

"Detective MacAlister, you'll have my report tomorrow. We're not going to be able to confirm anything else until the lab reports are back, and that will take several weeks."

Just what they needed. A conservative opinion.

"Good thing you need to sign a death certificate before you can release the body or we might not even have a cause of death," Vik said.

Dr. Nichols almost opened her mouth, but checked herself and said nothing.

Janet Petrosky was due back Wednesday night. Marti intended to call her first thing Thursday morning. Right now they had a seventy-year-old victim of asphyxia. The autopsy did not bear out his family's opinion that he was in poor health due to heart trouble and cancer. There was ulceration and hemorrhaging in his digestive tract, cause unknown, and she and Vik were going to have to determine whether or not that was important to their case.

As they left the building, Vik said, "It sure

would have been nice to know what the old lady was saying to Denise last night."

"Something about stealing and hats," Marti said.

"How do you know? That sure wasn't Spanish."

"No," Marti said. "It was Gullah. Gladys, or someone in the family, must come from South Carolina. They say it's derived from an original African dialect, and that's the only place I know of in this country where it's spoken."

"Wilke Co!" Vik said. *Big deal,* in Polish.

"Wein," Marti replied. *I know.*

Vik looked surprised.

"Yes," she told him, "I had a partner in Chicago who spoke Polish. I know when you're muttering curses and death threats."

As much as Marti had enjoyed keeping this from him, she had decided to tell him a few days ago, after his curses became more obscene than usual.

He headed for the car without answering.

CHAPTER

6

It was 10:15 when Marti pulled up in front of the Hamilton residence. She timed her visit to coincide with Sunday morning services at Mount Gethsemane, hoping to meet only with members of the family. Unlike last night, she didn't have any problem finding a place to park.

Vik had agreed that Marti would come here first and that he would follow in about half an hour with an evidence tech. It was a small, professional courtesy that might buffer the intrusion. They both remembered the cases Denise had helped them with, finding temporary shelter or foster care or counseling for the kids involved.

Marti glanced about as she headed up the walk. Two oak trees in the front yard with a few leaves left on the branches. Piles of brown leaves along the curb. No flower beds. She walked to the end of the driveway and looked into the yard. About two-thirds was black topsoil.

Denise answered the bell and stood silently for a moment. Her eyes looked tired, as if she hadn't had much sleep the night before. "'Morning, Mac-Alister. I don't suppose this is just routine."

Marti followed her to the kitchen and let her fix them both a cup of coffee, watching as Denise opened a cupboard, took down mismatched pink and green cups and saucers, then looked at them and tossed them into the wastebasket. She reached up to a higher shelf and chose two shiny, navy blue mugs instead.

"Black is fine," Marti said as Denise poured.

"They came for his pillows. What's the official cause of death?"

"Asphyxia, by suffocation."

Coffee sloshed over the sides of the mugs. Denise ignored it.

"Terri will really get upset now."

A curious response, Marti thought. "Do you know why anyone would want him dead?"

Denise almost smiled. It seemed closer to a grimace. "A good man like my stepfather? A deacon of the church? A God-fearing and upright man?" She brought the mugs to the table.

"Where were you Friday night and early Saturday morning?"

"I have no alibi, MacAlister, but I wasn't here, and I didn't kill him."

"I'd like to speak with your mother."

"Sure. She's taking a bath now."

"Alone," Marti added.

Denise sat across from her and added a packet of artificial sweetener to her coffee.

It was a small kitchen. The stove was old and the refrigerator hummed loudly. The wood floor showed through the blocks of red-and-white linoleum in several spots. The red poppy pattern on the curtains was faded. Except for a toaster, there were no small appliances on the counter. The coffeepot and a small pan on the stove were made of cheap aluminum, the pan dented.

Marti sipped the coffee. Caffeine was a poor second to a full night's sleep but would keep her awake and alert, at least until midafternoon.

Denise stared at her mug, rubbing the small gilt pattern with her index finger. "Strange. All of it. Strange his being dead." She pushed at the short, dark curls that framed her face. "They seem so . . . all-powerful when you're young. Invincible. Then you watch them get sick, get old."

Marti sat very still. There was an odd inflection in Denise's voice. She couldn't tell if it was relief, disappointment, surprise, or something else.

"Mother seems so fragile now," Denise went on. "Funny how you think that just because you're grown, you're independent of your mother, you don't need her, don't want her needing you. But it would be so difficult for either of us to get along without the other."

Marti thought of her own mother, in Arkansas, taking care of Aunt Cindy. She considered all of the times she needed to talk something over with Momma, but didn't call. She thought of what her own daughter Joanna, now fifteen, had missed by being so far away from the wisdom of that strong and gentle woman she was named for.

Denise put down her mug with a decisive thump. "I've never been on this side of a police investigation. I'm not sure what to say or ask as a family member because I've listened to other people in the same circumstances, knowing that someone was lying."

"Are you lying?" Marti asked.

Denise gave her a small, wry smile that seemed filled with secrets. "No. Not yet anyway."

Marti thought back to last night, remembered the anger she had sensed in Denise and hoped she was not involved in her stepfather's death. It had seemed almost as if Denise was the mother, not Gladys. And now, seeing the weary slump of Denise's shoulders and knowing how aloof she remained from everyone at work, she wondered who Denise turned to for comfort. Marti was already more personally involved in this case than she wanted to be and cared more about what happened to Denise than she should.

"Do you know of any reason why anyone would want to harm your stepfather?"

Denise looked at her with an expression that made her seem old. "Many."

"Would you care to elaborate?"

"No."

Marti didn't expect Denise to confide in her. "Why did you think he was ill?"

Denise looked puzzled. "It was obvious."

"Why?"

"He looked sick, acted sick. That old man wasn't putting us on, was he? If he was, it was wasted on me. I sure didn't feel sorry for him. But damn—Terri—if he put her through . . . no, Terri puts herself through . . . she wouldn't be happy if she didn't have something to be miserable about. He was sick, wasn't he?"

Marti didn't answer.

Denise rubbed her temples and slouched back in the chair. "We had to take him to the hospital half a dozen times in the past year and a half. They'd give him a follow-up appointment with a doctor, but he always refused to go. He was always so damned stubborn. He had an opinion about everything and never let anything change his mind."

"Why did he refuse to see a doctor?"

"He said he'd never been to a doctor in his life except for his army physicals and wasn't going to one of those quacks now so they could kill him before his time."

Denise smiled, almost derisively. "He said he'd die in God's time, not man's. I wonder if that's what this was? God's time. God's way. You're here investigating. Does that mean it was man's time? Or did they coincide?"

They were silent for a few minutes. Then Denise said, "I always did want a father when I was a little girl. All of the other kids I knew had one." She said it as casually as she might mention wanting a doughnut to dunk in her coffee, but Marti heard a hint of regret in her voice.

Whenever they had worked together on a case involving a juvenile, everything Denise did was unerringly correct. Marti suspected that like many gifts, Denise's skill with children came from some kind of personal pain.

Gladys Hamilton came into the room before they could say anything else. Denise poured a cup of coffee for her mother and excused herself. Gladys didn't look like she had gotten much sleep either. She moved as if her joints were stiff or her bones ached, and rubbed her index fingers along the sides of her nose. She was wearing a black jersey dress that emphasized how petite she was.

Marti waited until Gladys had added three spoonfuls of sugar and an equal amount of powdered creamer to her coffee. Then she said,

"Mrs. Hamilton. We have reason to believe that your husband didn't die from natural causes. He died of asphxiation. Someone suffocated him."

She waited for a reaction, saw nothing but the spoon making small circles in the cup.

Mrs. Hamilton sighed and spoke without looking up. "I thought he'd just die one day. I thought we would bury him, get on with our lives. It isn't going to be like that, is it?"

"How long were you married?"

"Thirty-five years come August. The church was planning something for us. There won't be any celebrating now."

Marti tried to ignore the clinking sound of metal against china. There was no sign of forced entry. Nothing was missing. It was unlikely that anyone, friend or stranger, had come into the house and killed Henry Hamilton. Logic, statistics, common sense, and the historical data on this type of homicide pointed to a member of the family. Gladys Hamilton was a tiny woman, but looked wiry and strong enough to straddle her sleeping husband and press a pillow on his face until he was dead. Marti had known smaller women who had done as much and more. Or had one of them held the pillow while the other pinned him down? There was no mistaking Denise and Gladys's ambivalence. She was catching glimpses of resentment and relief as well as sadness, and, she thought, genuine grief.

Gladys finally took the spoon out of her cup and placed it on the table. She looked at Marti. "Do you want me to weep? To mourn him? I do. But for my own reasons, not any that you would understand. It's hard crying for someone who left you years ago, or maybe wasn't ever there, except in your own mind's eye."

A sense of loss, Marti decided. That was the emotion that she hadn't been able to identify. There was a wistfulness in Gladys's voice that Marti had seen in Denise, both last night and again this morning.

As Gladys looked past Marti, toward the window, moisture gathered in her eyes until two tears made paths down her cheeks. She sniffled, took a handkerchief with tatted corners out of her pocket, and dried her eyes. Then she tossed her head as if to shake off the mood that had prompted her tears. "They came for his bed pillows."

"Yes, ma'am. And my partner and an evidence technician will be here in about five minutes to have a look around."

"A look around?" Gladys Hamilton said. "Poking and prying and snooping and asking all kinds of questions. Coming here like buzzards and by the time you're done you'll have picked at our bones. And all because of Henry." She looked at Marti with moist eyes. "And Henry," she said, her voice just above a whisper. "He'll be far from it all, same as always."

When Vik came in, Marti gave him a small shake of her head to indicate that she hadn't gotten any information from either woman. Vik took out his notebook and pulled up one of the kitchen chairs. He pushed back a straying strand of hair that sprang back as soon as he took his hand away. There was something boyish in the gesture that made the fierceness of his craggy features seem less intense. His habitual scowl became earnest.

"I'm Detective Jessenovik, ma'am. I need to ask you a few questions."

Undistracted by Vik, Gladys watched as the evidence tech passed through the kitchen, heading for her husband's bedroom.

"What are you going to go through?" she called.

"No more than what's necessary, ma'am."

Denise came into the kitchen. "Let it be, Momma. They're just doing their job. Be all right." She leaned against a counter, arms folded.

"Mrs. Hamilton," Vik said. "Did anything at all happen last week that was unusual? Did your husband complain to a neighbor about a barking dog, yell at the paperboy for not delivering a paper? Have an argument with a friend? Anything at all out of the ordinary?"

Gladys shook her head.

"Could you tell me everything your husband did Friday, ma'am. Or as much as you know or can remember."

"He didn't do anything that was any different from what he did every other day for the past five or six years. Once he retired he didn't do much of anything except for church work, fishing, and gardening, things he enjoyed."

"What did he do Friday?" Vik asked.

Gladys thought for a minute. "He got up at six-thirty, same as always. He had to have his coffee before he got dressed and he didn't like sitting around in his bathrobe. I fixed oatmeal and stewed prunes for breakfast, same as always."

"Who has keys to the house, besides you and him?"

"Denise, and my sister Dolly."

"Keys to the front and back doors?"

"Just the front."

"And nobody else has a key? No friends or other relatives? Neither of your other daughters?"

"Nobody else."

"You sleep in the front bedroom, ma'am. Your husband's room is in the back. Would you have heard someone if they came in through the back door?"

Gladys shrugged, thought for a moment, then shook her head. "No, I don't think so."

"But if someone came through the front door, you would have heard them."

"I didn't hear anything." She pressed her hands together, then rubbed the sides of her nose again. "Lord, Denise, how many times am I going to have to say all of this?"

Denise pulled up a chair and sat beside her. She took her mother's hands, covering them with her own. "You're going to answer these questions. We'll worry about the other times when we come to them. There might not be another time. Nobody is going to harass you. They're just doing what has to be done."

Gladys nodded. "Didn't nothing much of anything happen last week. Nothing that was different from any other week since Henry retired. Didn't nothing much of anything ever happen around here."

"He'd been in poor health for a while, hadn't he, ma'am? It must have been difficult for you, looking after him."

Gladys nodded.

"But he wasn't seeing a doctor?"

"Wouldn't go near one. Not since he got out of the army."

"Did he take any over-the-counter medications?"

"Some of everything. Here, I'll show you."

Gladys opened one of the kitchen cabinets the uniform had missed. She was right. Henry had taken a wide variety of nonprescribed medicine, and just about everything on the market for stomach and intestinal distress.

"Was he ever irritable?" Vik asked.

"Most of the time."

"Figures. Medicine seems harmless enough when you can get it without a prescription, but if you mix the wrong stuff together, you can have a serious reaction. Irritability is a common symptom of that."

Marti was going to remember that the next time Vik got cranky, probably by tomorrow.

Vik rubbed his chin and Marti took over.

"Did you notice anything unusual when you brought him his coffee Saturday morning?" she asked.

Gladys sighed, didn't answer.

"Ma'am, how was he when you went into his room Saturday morning?" she persisted. According to the autopsy, Henry had died between one and four o'clock Saturday morning. The woman must have known something was wrong.

Gladys gave Marti a stern look as if reprimanding her for being sassy, or maybe just reminding her that they were both black and had both been raised to be deferential to older folk. Marti shrugged off the emotional response that suggested that Gladys was right.

"Did you bring your husband his coffee on Saturday morning, Mrs. Hamilton?" she asked, her voice as courteous as she could manage without letting the older woman get the upper hand.

"No. I looked in on him first. Then, when I saw he was still sleeping, I went out."

"You left the house without fixing his coffee?" Marti asked.

Gladys's chin tilted at a defiant angle. Her eyes were bright with anger.

"I told you. Yes."

Denise patted her mother's hands. Gladys looked at her daughter as if she had forgotten she was there, then seemed to relax a little.

"How often did he sleep past six-thirty?" Marti asked.

"Not lately. Not that I can recall."

"When was the last time your husband was still sleeping when you left the house?"

Denise cautioned her mother with a hand on her arm. "MacAlister, she's answering your questions as best she can."

Marti swore to herself. Denise shouldn't be here.

Mrs. Hamilton looked from one of them to the other, then said, "I can't remember the last time Henry slept that late."

"Did you think something might be wrong?"

Gladys shrugged. "Contrary old man, that

Henry. I thought maybe he was faking so he'd have something to complain about later on."

Denise suggested that her mother should lie down, and Marti agreed. Vik, unable to restrain himself, went to Henry's room to supervise the tech.

Denise clasped her neck with both hands, pacing and massaging her neck at the same time. When she reached the window, she turned. "This isn't how I expected it to be when he was gone. I thought it would be over."

"Thought what would be over?"

Denise shook her head.

"For the record," Marti said, "where were you from twelve-thirty Friday night until six-thirty Saturday morning?"

Denise didn't seem surprised by the question. "Sometimes, when I can't sleep, I go to the lake, sit there for a while. Friday night I drove up to a place I like in Racine. I left about midnight and didn't get back until about three."

"Anyone see you?"

"I doubt it. If they did I can't think of any reason why they'd remember." Denise yawned.

The evidence tech motioned to them from the doorway and they followed him into Hamilton's bedroom.

"I've got prints from the window casing that I estimate could have been there anywhere from two hours to thirty-six hours based on the amount of moisture. And I checked the doors. They've got a dead bolt, a strike bar, and a chain on the front door, and a doorknob lock on the back door. I got in by giving the back door a hard shove without doing any damage. I opened it with a credit card, too. Interesting thing, though. I lifted some prints off the inside of the back door, but the outside is so clean someone could have wiped it down."

Vik shrugged. Marti nodded. Anyone could have come in.

C H A P T E R
7

It was a little before one in the afternoon when Denise arrived at Whittaker's Funeral Home. She spoke briefly with Ezra's mother, then went downstairs to the basement showroom where the caskets were kept. Thank God Momma had decided to have the funeral right away, even if it was only because she didn't want to deal with the old man's family. She paused as she heard Terri's voice.

"Look, Momma, velvet lining. How soft. Daddy would like that. Can't you just see his head on the pillow?"

"That casket is pink," Belle said.

"No, it's not," Terri said. "It's beige."

"Pink," Belle insisted. "We want something that looks like wood. What the hell do they make these things out of, anyway? I bet it's plastic. They make damned near everything out of some kind of plastic these days." Denise heard a knocking sound. "Here. This will do. Mahogany. Solid. Distinguished. Dignified. Just like Daddy, don't you think?"

"Belle, I don't think we need you to help pick out Daddy's casket," Terri said. "You don't even have enough taste to wear a decent dress on a Sunday afternoon. You look like you're going barhopping."

"I've already been barhopping."

"Belle, for God's sake. Can't you leave that booze alone for one day? Just to show a little respect for the dead? It's not even one o'clock yet. You can't do anything without a drink, can you?"

"Why would I want to?"

Denise sat down on the steps and put her head in her hands. What was going to happen to them with the old man dead? Momma wouldn't have anyone but her and Aunt Dolly. Maybe, since Aunt Dolly was a widow too, they would spend more time together. Or maybe Momma would make more demands on her. With Daddy gone, she wasn't even sure that Terri would come to the house. And when Belle did show up, always unannounced and inebriated, she wasn't any help at all.

"Momma," Terri said. "What's he going to wear? We should coordinate the casket with his suit. He loved that light gray one. And the beige. Those were his favorites."

"Poor old fool," Belle said. "Have they brought him here yet? Is he in another room somewhere getting all of his blood drained out? Does Ezra do that himself, or does he let the little woman help out? Hey, maybe you can put on Daddy's makeup, or stuff his cheeks with a little cotton."

"Oh God," Terri cried. "My daddy. He's dead. I'll never see him again. Never. He'll never see my little baby boy. Oh, God, why?"

"Oh, Terri," Belle said. "Don't start that 'my daddy' shit again, I heard enough of that last night. Save it for the funeral. If you hadn't taken him to that stupid faith healer he'd be here right now. You just remember that. It's your fault that he's dead."

"Belle," Momma said. "Terri loved him."

"And I didn't?" Belle said. "She loved him, but not me? Nobody knows how I feel about anything. Nobody cares."

"There you go," Terri said. "Feeling sorry for yourself."

"Me? Listen, little sister, I didn't have no silver spoon in my mouth like you did. Nobody gave a damn if I wanted music lessons or voice training. But you—ballet, tap, piano, guitar, proms, a cotillion."

"By the time you were old enough for a cotillion, Belle, you were drinking too much to be trusted to even show up. You got drunk at your freshman turnabout. Daddy couldn't even trust you with a house key. Not after you stole his watch."

"You took that damned watch, Terri, and blamed it on me."

Denise wished that she could leave, wished that just for once, Momma would shut the two of them up.

"Strumpet, that's what he called you," Terri said. "I was his little girl."

"You killed him," Belle insisted. "You and that damned faith healer and maybe even your boyfriend."

Terri began sobbing. "Why do you always have to tell such horrible lies about me? I loved him more than anybody else in the whole world. Momma, do you hear what she's saying about me? You've got some nerve, Belle. You couldn't even show up sober enough to help pick out a casket."

Denise felt like screaming. Why didn't they just shut up? Not even his death could stop them. An hour from now they would still be going at it. Momma would be wringing her hands with that long-suffering look on her face. It would be left up to her to decide which casket they'd bury him in. It was always going to be like this. Nothing was ever going to change.

CHAPTER 8

On Sunday afternoon Marti went to see the Reverend Douglas, pastor of Mount Gethsemane. Because the most likely suspects at this point were members of the family, she would have to begin with people on the perimeter of their lives and work her way in. She wouldn't have much more to say to Gladys and her daughters until she knew a lot more about them. She also needed to know more about the victim. The Reverend Douglas seemed to be a good person to start with because both Hamiltons were active members of the church.

The Douglases lived on the northeast side of town in a large Victorian house. A Lincoln Continental was parked in one side of the open two-car garage that had once housed horse-drawn carriages. Three bicycles, a wagon, and several skateboards cluttered the remaining space.

As she went up the walk, Marti looked in the windows. A white dove in a large hanging cage stared back at her.

The reverend opened the door. He had what Marti liked to call presence. He was tall and broad-shouldered, his skin a smooth walnut brown. His eyes were dark and brooding, but there were laugh crinkles at the corners. He was dressed casually, in jeans and a fishermen's knit sweater. The only indication of his age, which was close to fifty, was the gray hair at his temples.

"Sister MacAlister. Come right in." His smile was rueful. "I don't suppose this is just a friendly visit, not with the police at Brother Hamilton's house last night and today. Do you mind coming into the kitchen?"

He led the way down a narrow hall. "My wife is still at church. She shouldn't be much longer if you want to speak with her."

There was a thumping above their heads. "No wrestling up there!" he yelled.

"The twins," he said to Marti. "Seven going on twenty-eight, and my other five are so much older they spoil them rotten. You'll have to make do with my coffee. I sure miss having my Melissa around. She's a freshman at Eastern Michigan."

The kitchen reminded Marti of her grandmother's—roomy, with a pantry and odd nooks and crannies built into the walls. The cabinets were painted blue. The table was round and the wooden chairs had thick, ruffled cushions. Magnets held school papers to the refrigerator door.

The Reverend Douglas seemed right at home, assembling cups and saucers while water seeped through the filter and coffee dripped into the pot. He pushed aside a pile of coloring books and cut thick slices of pound cake. "I made this myself. It's one of my mother's recipes, Lord rest her soul."

Marti caught just a whiff of lemon and considered the calories without guilt.

"Now, Sister MacAlister," the reverend said, sitting down. "How can I help you?"

"Mr. Hamilton's death has been ruled a homicide."

"I was afraid of that when you called. I suppose the next question is if I know of anyone who might have done it."

"Maybe," Marti said. "Or why. What I'd really like you to do is just tell me about Mr. Hamilton."

The Reverend Douglas leaned back, folding his arms. Wide-spaced, dark eyebrows hunched closer together as he looked at her. "For some reason I expected you to ask me about his family."

"I'll get around to that." If anyone was going to point her toward the person who did this, it would most likely be the victim.

"Henry Hamilton," the reverend mused. "He helped my daddy build this church. Kept the books from day one, while he was still working at American Motors full time. He was treasurer until he died."

"An honest man?"

"I sure hope so." The reverend chuckled. "I can't make heads nor tails out of the way he kept the books. Sister Newman is going to take over now. She's a CPA. Now that we're going to build a school we'll need an accountant to oversee things. I tried, tactfully, to get Henry to step down, but with his health failing and all, I think it was important to him to feel useful. And perhaps he needed the money we paid him, once he retired. He did ask if Sister Holmes could help out. But I think the most she did was type the checks and make bank deposits."

"What aren't you telling me?"

Instead of answering, the reverend stood and called upstairs. "Aaron? Timothy? Awfully quiet up there!"

"We're playing Battleship!"

Returning to his chair, he said, "Brother Hamilton was very reserved. A somber man, not given to laughter or humor. He and my daddy worked together for years, but they were not close. I couldn't have run the church without him when I first took over, but he kept his distance with me, too."

"Did he participate in social activities?"

"He usually attended, along with Gladys and her sister, Dolly, until he became ill. And when the girls were children, all three of them were active. Denise still is. Terri comes when she can."

"Did he have any close friends among the members?"

"He seemed to be on good terms with everybody. He just kept to himself. You might talk to Brother Franklin, our head deacon, or Brother Gilmore. Those three have worked together for the church since before the cornerstone was laid. There wouldn't be a Mount Gethsemane without them."

"What's your opinion of Henry Hamilton?"

He thought for a minute. "It bothers me that he has done so much for the church but the church seems to have done so little for him." He spoke slowly, considering his words. "There's the person who has the spirit of charity, and the person who just gives and gives. I suppose it's easy enough to confuse the two. Henry Hamilton was the latter. His help was invaluable, and I more than appreciate everything he did. It just troubles me sometimes that we did not do more for him."

He leaned back and put both hands palms down on the table. "As for Gladys, I don't know. From the time they got married it seemed like she was here more than home. Women run this church. The Marthas and Marys, praying and working, are our backbone, our strength, our support, our survival. My wife, Esther, has a ministry now called Martha's Table. It's for women who spend too much time at church, not enough time at home. Now we recognize that when they're here as often as Gladys was, something isn't right in their lives. Back then, we had Women's Day the second Sunday in August and gave them annual awards. Esther has tried numerous times to bring Gladys out, get her to talk more. We're concerned that something is troubling her, but like Henry, Gladys keeps to herself."

He cut two more slices of pound cake. "I always assumed Gladys became so active in the church because she was excluded, or excluded herself, before her marriage. Denise and Belle were born out of wedlock. All the members the Hamiltons' age know it, although it's not spoken of now. Everyone thought highly of Henry for making an honest woman of Gladys. There was a major stigma attached to having babies without benefit of marriage back then." He smiled. "We're supposed to overlook the fact that most of the social and religious amenities are ignored these days, like marriage first, then living together, then children."

"Did Gladys and Henry meet at church?"

He thought for a minute. "I can't say. I was a lot younger then, too. Now that I think about it, I remember people saying Henry was intending to marry someone else and Gladys came along and stole his heart, or something equally romantic. Daddy's not here to ask, but I seem to recall something like that. Sister Hannah Hardy would know. Ninety if she's a day but comes to church most every Sunday that the weather's decent. We've got some of the younger ones taking down an oral history from her. She knows a lot that we ought not forget."

Marti was at her desk polishing off a Big Mac and a side of fries when Vik came in. They shared an office on the southwest side of the precinct with two Vice cops who worked Saturday night and usually didn't come in on Sunday. With four desks and a table big enough for a coffeemaker, a doughnut box, and the manual typewriter they all shared, the room wasn't crowded. It was a big change from the cramped quarters she used to work out of in Chicago.

Vik was frowning as he draped his coat over the back of his chair. He looked into his Chicago Bears Super Bowl mug, which was chipped but irreplaceable. Without speaking, he fed the dregs of his coffee to the spider plant. Then he looked inside the McDonald's bag on Marti's desk and extracted one of two apple pies.

"I'll bet you're missing out on a great home-cooked meal, MacAlister, spinach and tofu casserole. You owe me one for not telling Joanna about this."

Joanna, Marti's fifteen-year-old daughter, had lost her father in the line of duty, and to compensate for her lack of control over that, was doing her best to keep her surviving parent healthy.

"I think things are beginning to even out, Vik. We had a turkey roast and mashed potatoes with our salad last night, and bean pie for dessert." It was almost five o'clock now, and she hadn't written any reports on the Hamilton homicide yet. She had to track down Belle as well, and try to see Terri. By the time she got home it would be time for her ten-year-old son Theo to go to bed.

"That dinner sounds almost normal after broccoli lasagna and green bean pizza," Vik agreed, holding out his mug for some of her milk shake. "All we got from a canvass of the neighborhood was one retiree who heard a car stop near his house at about three o'clock Saturday morning. He insists that he wrote down the license plate number but he can't remember where he put the piece of paper. I don't believe him. There's no way he could see that good."

"That's within range of time of death. Did you get a description?"

"Come on, Marti, this isn't 'Dragnet.' The old guy spent twenty minutes explaining what was wrong with his eyesight, then he said he was sure the car was dark. It could have been black, brown, gray, blue, or green, but it was dark. It was either a two-door or a four-door. No guess as to the year, make, or model, but it looked like one of those foreign cars. The one thing he is sure of is that it did not belong in the neighborhood. We checked and no one in a three-block radius says they had any visitors at that hour."

"That's better than nothing."

"Not by a hell of a lot."

"Where does this guy live?" Marti asked.

"Around the corner, a block over."

"Did he see anyone in the car, or leaving it?"

"Of course not. He didn't hear a door open or close. He says he sat by the window for a while to make sure nobody was casing the neighborhood or breaking and entering. He dozed off after about half an hour. He didn't hear the car leave. His house is about midblock. He says that if anyone cut through any of the yards, several dogs would have barked."

"Sounds like he took his time getting out of bed after he heard the car stop."

"This guy is old, real old," Vik said. "Eighty-five maybe. He probably got out of bed as fast as he could."

"Which could mean ten or twenty minutes. He

could have some problems with perceptions of time, too," Marti said. "Might have watched out the window a couple of minutes and dozed off right away."

"I told you we didn't have a lot, Marti."

"Depends. Maybe he did see a vehicle. Maybe the time he observed is correct. If so, the question is why was the car there, and did it have anything to do with Hamilton's death. What's the beat cop say?"

"No observation on the car, but he did see a man out walking his dog about two A.M."

"Terrific. Was the dog male or female?"

Vik broke off a piece of the apple pie. It was still too hot to eat. "I don't like this one," he said. "I don't like Denise Stevens's involvement."

"Not much we can do about that, Jessenovik."

Marti told him what little she had gleaned from the Reverend Douglas. "We've got court tomorrow. I can start interviewing after that. I want to talk with the two deacons first, Franklin and Gilmore, and I haven't been able to get in touch with either one of them. Did you get any kind of a feel for the Hamiltons as a couple while you were canvassing?"

"They kept pretty much to themselves. She canned or froze most of the produce from their garden and gave the rest away. He paid two teenagers who live a couple of houses down to handle minor chores—snow shoveling, taking out the garbage, mowing the lawn, some of the yard work. Both boys said Hamilton never talked to them, unless he wasn't satisfied with their work. I got the impression that might have happened pretty often. They seemed to like Mrs. Hamilton, though, said she always had something she'd baked and hot or cold drinks when they were finished. They said she never talked much, either." His chair squeaked as he leaned back and put his hands behind his head. "So much for today's snooping. Before it's over I bet we're going to find out a lot of things we'll wish we didn't have to know."

Like Vik, Marti didn't care much for this kind of case. It was much easier to forget what you found out about the deceased than it was to forget what you knew about the living, especially if you continued to see or work with them.

"We'd better be careful not to assume that this is a domestic homicide, Vik, even though it does look that way."

"Right," Vik agreed. "One homicide. One weapon, a pillow. That doesn't sound like something Denise would do."

It was worrying him. "No, it doesn't," Marti agreed. "But she doesn't have much of an alibi, Vik, if it ever comes down to that."

They both knew that given the right circumstances or provocation, people would do just about anything.

It was after ten when Marti found Belle in a small bar on the South Side.

"Where was I when the old bastard died?" Belle's speech was slurred and she squinted as she tried to focus on Marti. "With him." She indicated a tall, thin man sitting beside her. "Right, honey?"

The man nodded. He was as drunk as Belle.

"Wanna know what we were doin'?"

The man leered at Belle.

"It got good to you, didn't it, baby."

Marti settled for the name of the motel they stayed at. She felt depressed as she left. She would have to check out Terri's alibi after court tomorrow. According to Ezra, Terri was too upset right now to see her. He said he and Terri were together at home on Friday night.

CHAPTER

9

As soon as Ezra fell asleep watching the ten o'clock news, Terri went to the window. She pulled the curtain back just enough to peek out. The car that had followed them home from the filling station this morning was parked across the street. She could see the tip of a cigarette glowing in the dark. It looked like the man who had smiled at her while Ezra was paying for the gas was waiting outside for her now, even though she had rolled down the window and told him she was married and couldn't go with him. He had seemed surprised she felt that way, but he had said, "Sure, lady, whatever you say," as if he understood. Now he expected her to leave Ezra and run away with him. Why was this always happening to her? Even men she saw on the street and at the grocery store wanted her to be with them, wanted her to leave Ezra for them.

Turning, she looked at Ezra, slack-jawed and snoring. He'd wake up in a couple of hours and go to his room, not hers, because she was pregnant. If she awakened him, told him about the man waiting outside, he'd say she was making it up, that the car belonged to a neighbor. She eased the door open so Ezra's mother wouldn't hear, and kept to the side of the hall where the floor didn't creak. When she reached the kitchen, the only light came from the open refrigerator.

Danzel, Ezra's hearse driver, opened the drawer where the meat was kept. There was a can of beer on the counter. Danzel was kin to Ezra and had the run of the house. He was as tall as Daddy, and lean and light-skinned, too. He had a look in his eyes, as if he could see for miles and miles and years and years. He kissed better than anyone else she knew.

"There's no cheese," she said.

He jumped. "Terri!"

She smiled. "We ran out, but there's a jar of cheese spread." He was so helpless sometimes.

She got out the cheese spread, a loaf of bread, and the Wisconsin sausage she always kept for him. She stuck her finger in the jar. "Here, have a snack while you're waiting."

Danzel licked the cheese from her finger.

"I would give you another little snack, but you're greedy."

When the sandwich was ready she popped open the can of beer and poured some into a glass. She held the glass to his lips.

Danzel took a sip, then put his arms around her. "You okay, baby?"

"Now I am," she said. Poor Danzel. He couldn't keep his hands off her. Few men could. "He's outside," she told him.

"Who is it this time?"

"He followed me home from the filling station."

Danzel laughed softly. It reminded her of a cat purring. "That's what happens when you're irresistible, baby. After a couple of nights he'll realize you're not interested and go away. All the others have."

"But there will be more."

Danzel stroked her hair. "Yes," he agreed. "There will always be more."

At least he believed her. "I didn't feel safe here until you came. Now you're here to stop them if they try to come in and make me go away with them."

"You're not going anywhere, baby. Not until you leave here with me. And with your daddy's funeral Tuesday, and the baby due next month, it won't be long."

But she didn't want to go away with him, either. She wanted Danzel to stay here, to protect her, to love her the way Ezra couldn't love her very often. She couldn't leave. Maybe she should have told him that, but once he found out she was having his baby, he started talking about the three of them moving out. She didn't even love him. Sometimes, when she was with him, she pretended he was someone else.

"Ezra won't let me see Daddy. You have the keys. Take me downstairs."

"I don't have the keys. Ezra took them this morning. Sorry, baby, but there was nothing I could do. You're not going to see your daddy until the wake tomorrow night."

"Is he really dead? Are they just telling me he is to keep me from ever seeing him again? Have you seen him?"

"I haven't seen him yet."

"Then it must not be true. It's a trick. Where have they taken him? Momma put him in a nursing home, didn't she? Or she took him to a doctor and he's in the hospital and they've operated and—"

"Hey, hey. Don't get upset. Stay calm. You'll wake Ezra up, or his mother. Shhh."

She leaned against him. "They wouldn't let me see him last night, either."

"Terri, the police were there. They said that he didn't die because he was sick, that someone did it."

"No. That's not true. They're wrong."

"Half the choir saw him. Come on, baby, he's gone."

"But I don't want him to be."

"Well, I thought you did."

"Danzel!" She pulled away from him. "I loved him. I'm the only one who loved him and I'm the only one he loved."

"Hey, baby, I know that, but now that he's gone, you've got all that insurance money, and we can leave here, the three of us. We can open up that record shop like we've been planning to. We can be a family just like we talked about."

Terri backed away from him, confused. *He* had said that. *He* had wanted that. Not her. She just didn't want to be so alone here.

"Hey, Terri, baby. He was sick. You know that. You didn't really want him to keep suffering like that, did you? He's better off now."

How could Daddy be better off if it meant being away from her? How could Danzel even think she wanted Daddy to die? Was it her fault that Daddy was dead—hers and Danzel's? She turned and hurried from the room.

C H A P T E R
10

Gladys pulled all the curtains shut and turned on every light in the house. Maybe nobody else would stop by. Maybe there wouldn't be any more gifts of food to be put into the freezer. Maybe they would leave her alone. Just for tonight.

She hadn't known how quiet it would be without Henry, or how clearly she would hear everything he could no longer say. She wanted to take off her felt slippers and put on the shoes she bought yesterday and listen to them click on the parquet floor, hoping they made little scratches. All she could hear was Henry, warning her not to. Would he never leave her?

She got a box of garbage bags and went into his room. Denise said she would help get his clothes packed away, but Gladys couldn't wait. She didn't care how it looked if she got rid of his things so soon. Too bad it would be another week before that veterans' group could come for his furniture. She wished she could just tear down this room. She went to the closet first, laid his shirts and ties and suits across the bed, folded each as she put them into the bags. Henry had his suits made special. His shirts had monograms. His jewelry was real silver, real gold. Nothing was too good for old Henry. She put the navy blue pinstripe to one side, along with a white shirt. She'd told Ezra everything was too big now, but Ezra said they'd make it all fit him okay when they laid him out.

Socks, no shoes. The gray-and-red tie. Gladys smoothed and folded and arranged everything else in the bags. Denise said she'd take it all to the Salvation Army men's shelter. And there was his army trunk in the basement. Should she go through it first, or just send it along? Maybe there were papers in it, things she should burn and not give away. She would save that for later.

She looked about the room. His jewelry should go to the deacons, she thought. He had no friends. She had no friends. She had called Reverend Douglas tonight. The funeral would be held on Tuesday. Too soon, he said, not enough time for people who lived out of state to make travel arrangements. She didn't want Henry's family to come.

Bootsie came in, rubbing against her legs and

making little meowing noises that sounded like questions. Gladys wasn't sure who had been the happiest when Bootsie showed up at the back door today. Poor thing had been out for two nights. Henry had forgotten to let her in Friday night and she hadn't even thought about her last night. Gladys picked up the cat and closed the door on her way out. Tomorrow, she thought, stroking soft fur. Tomorrow all of Henry's things would be out of here. Maybe then the sound of his voice would be gone.

She didn't care how it looked, getting rid of his things so soon. Who would see his room to know? When she reached the kitchen, Bootsie jumped from her arms and returned to Henry's door, meowing and pacing, expecting him to let her in.

"He's not here," Gladys scolded. "And you had best be getting used to that. It's just you and me here now. Henry's not here anymore."

But in her mind's eye she could almost see him standing in the doorway, scolding because the dishes hadn't been washed yet, calling her a slut, his pet name for her when they were alone. He had spit on her again last Wednesday.

She changed into her nightgown, put on a heavy robe, and turned down the heat. After she made a cup of chamomile tea, she remembered that she could turn up the heat as high as she wanted and adjusted the thermostat. Then she went into the living room, chose the chair in the corner, and tucked an afghan around her legs. She waited, half expecting Henry to complain about the lights and order the heat turned down.

She had never truly loved him. All these years, and not once had he said he loved her. Not once had she been held or comforted with love. She had thought an affection would develop between them, that a caring would grow as they got older. But always, he held himself away.

She had not come to this marriage blind. He had not wanted a wife, although in their younger years she bore him a daughter.

She had wanted Joe Nathan, Denise and Belle's father, but he remained out of reach. She had wanted everyone to stop laughing behind her back and mocking her love for Joe Nathan. She had wanted her mother to look at her and smile like she did when she looked at Dolly. She had wanted to protect her daughters. She had wanted them to have a father when they went to school. Somewhere, in some hidden place, she had believed that despite her reasons and his reasons, somewhere along the way something good would come of it.

Each spring they sowed the garden and each fall they harvested its yield. But for all of that growing, nothing ever grew between them that was good. Nothing good could ever come from him, not even now.

C H A P T E R

11

Late Monday afternoon, Marti and Vik arrived at Whittaker's Funeral Home, a spacious, two-story frame house. Ezra's grandfather had been the first black mortician in Lincoln Prairie, establishing a small storefront on Eureka Street, then part of a bustling downtown business district. Within five years of inheriting the family business, Ezra built this house.

There weren't any other cars in the parking lot, so Marti assumed that the family hadn't arrived. Rain streamed down the windshield and beat in irregular rhythms on the roof. At least it wasn't snow—that was what most people said this time of year. But she liked snow.

"Good thing you read the obituary in the *News-Times* while court was in recess or we wouldn't have known the wake was tonight."

"I wasn't expecting them to bury him any

sooner than Friday," Marti said. "There are relatives in South Carolina and Alabama. Some had to drive."

As she spoke a black Lexus pulled in. A woman Marti recognized as Gladys's sister, Dolly, got out first and put up an umbrella. Denise got out on the driver's side, saw Marti and Vik, and gave them a small wave. Tight-lipped, she assisted her mother out of the car.

Gladys Hamilton looked fragile as she leaned against Denise, buffeted by the wind. Gladys glanced in Marti's direction, then turned up the collar of her gray chesterfield and went inside flanked by Dolly and Denise. Dolly was about six inches taller than Gladys, and Denise was taller than both of them.

"We're going to have to talk with Denise about where she was at three o'clock Saturday morning," Vik said. He had been incredulous when the neighbor who reported seeing the car had called in with a license plate number that turned out to be hers. "He must have seen her car dozens of times."

"When he told you about the car he didn't associate it with the Hamiltons. And when he called, you asked him what *his* license plate number was and he couldn't tell you. I'm sure he didn't know Denise's."

"Damn." Vik ran his fingers through his hair. He'd rushed to the barbershop as soon as the judge recessed for lunch and it was short enough so that it wasn't too unruly. "We'll have to find out where Denise will be when this is over."

The parking lot was filling up. Marti recognized more people than she expected to. She hadn't known any of them two years ago. Funny, the way a place became home. When people began to park on the street, they decided it was time to go in. Vik gave her a pained look as he opened the car door and muttered, "I can hear them already."

He couldn't really, but by the time they reached the door it was obvious that Terri was "showing out" tonight.

"My daddy. My daddy."

"I'm not sure I can stand two hours of this," Vik said.

"My daddy," Terri sobbed.

"What do you think about Terri?" Vik asked.

"Believable," Marti said.

"You buy it?"

"No."

"I wonder where Belle is."

Marti was wondering too. "Probably getting drunk."

Gladys Hamilton was sitting in the vestibule accepting condolences Dolly was with her. Gladys was dry-eyed and calm. She was wearing a black suit that looked new and a high-collared, white silk blouse. Back straight, head erect, chin up, hand extended, she looked almost regal. A small, black pillbox hat with a wisp of a veil was perched on her head like a crown. Born to it, Momma would say. She used to say that widowhood suits some women; they manage it better than being married.

When they went to her, Vik mumbled "Mrs. Hamilton," and moved away. Marti thought she should say more, but had no idea what. When Gladys Hamilton looked at her, there was no pain, no hostility. She looked like someone whose burdens had been lifted. Marti squeezed Gladys's hand and said nothing.

Denise was greeting people as they entered the viewing room. Without hesitating, she turned to Marti and Vik, extended her hand, and said, "It was good of you to come." Looking away, Denise greeted the person behind them.

Terri was prostrate on a settee, sobbing loudly. A church sister in white uniform and nurse's cap sat with her. Ezra Whittaker was standing by the casket, eyes downcast, hands clasped behind his back, wearing the same bland expression he wore when he walked behind a casket during the procession into the church. He seemed to be ignoring his young wife. Marti did catch a few surreptitious glances at the deceased and a momentary impression of pride in his work.

Marti stayed away from the casket, to the rear of the room; not pretending to be anything other than what she was—a homicide detective, and conspicuously so. Her presence might be unnerving to whoever killed him. Although there was adequate seating, at least a hundred people stood about in small groups. She acknowledged those who spoke and tried not to smile at a few remarks about the police not having any respect for the dead.

Marti moved closer to the casket. Flocked, cream-colored wallpaper met oak wainscoting midpoint between ceiling and floor. Thick, maroon carpeting complemented maroon velvet drapes. The door fixtures, vases, and chandeliers were brass, the lighting near the casket was indirect. The floral arrangements were elaborate and ostentatious. One, with red roses and white carnations, had a ribbon that said MY DADDY.

Instead of lying flat, the deceased was turned slightly toward the viewers. There was a hint of a smile on his face, as if his passing had been pleasant. Marti remembered the position of his head on his pillow.

"My daddy," Terri moaned. For the most part, everyone left her alone.

There was a sudden silence, then Marti heard Belle. "My daddy! Where is he? Where they got my daddy laid out?"

Belle flounced into the room with an exaggerated strut, wobbling as she took long steps in spike heels, her red dress straining at the seams as she headed for the casket. A short, balding man jogged beside her as he tried to keep up, hold on to her elbow, and push at his eyeglasses all at once, without losing his balance when she staggered. Belle stopped abruptly when she was close enough to touch the casket. The little man lurched against her, and she reached for a flower stand to remain upright.

Ezra caught the flowers before they could fall, causing Belle to sway into the little man, who clutched at a handle on the casket. Ezra grabbed the man's elbow and escorted him to a chair while keeping a firm grip on Belle's arm.

Once the man was settled, Belle pulled Ezra back to the casket.

"Well, now," Belle said, loud but not belligerent. "Ain't we done my daddy up right proper. Did Terri help with the makeup? There's a little too much foundation on his forehead. And Momma must have picked out that suit. The only time he wore it was when everything else was at the cleaner's."

Belle took a step back, pulling Ezra with her. "My daddy," she said. "That's my daddy you got laying there dead." She patted Ezra on the back. "He sure looks one helluva lot better dead than he did the last time I saw him alive." Throwing her head back, she laughed, then put her head on Ezra's shoulder and started to cry. Unlike Terri's, Belle's sobs didn't sound phony at all.

When Gladys came into the room, she seemed dwarfed by Denise and Dolly on either side of her. Church members pressed her hand and murmured condolences as the women made their way to the casket. Gladys looked down at Henry for several minutes. Tears began streaming down her face as she said to Dolly, "I guess we just got each other now."

She smoothed the lapels on the suit, then touched Henry's cheek. Bending over, she kissed his forehead. Then she let Dolly lead her to a chair near the casket. Her shoulders shook as she cried.

"Well?" Vik asked.

"Looks convincing," Marti admitted.

"Believe it?"

"Get serious."

After the wake, Marti and Vik went to the church hall. The membership had outdone itself. Bowls and platters, casseroles and warming trays piled high with food crowded the tables that ran the length of the room. Members of the youth groups dispensed hot and cold drinks and replenished the paper plates, napkins, and plastic tableware.

Vik filled his plate with fried chicken, ham, baked macaroni, candied yams, and pie. "Is this bean pie?" he asked Marti.

"No, sweet potato."

"It's good. Do you ever make it? Or Joanna?"

"Just for the holidays."

"You could bring some to work."

"I'll remember that," Marti said, smiling. "Try some of those black-eyed peas and some collard greens."

She began another circuit of the room. Terri was sitting in an easy chair with her feet propped up on a folding chair. Her eyes were swollen and red, her stomach huge, her ankles and hands puffy. Ezra kept his distance. Marti wondered why.

Gladys was talking with Deacon Gilmore. He was bending down, with his mouth close to her ear and his hand on her arm. As Marti watched, Gladys pointed to one of the church women, pushed his hand off her arm, and walked away. Gilmore just stood there. When one of the other deacons approached him, Gilmore was looking at Gladys so intently that the other man had to tap him on the shoulder to get his attention.

Belle hadn't arrived yet, if she planned to. Denise was everywhere, smiling, talking, steering new arrivals to the buffet.

Marti had identified two older men, both light-skinned and tall, as relatives of the deceased. She was eating banana pudding when they came over to her.

The taller of the two spoke first. He looked younger than Henry, about Gladys's age. "They say you're one of the officers on this case."

"Yes, sir. How can I help you?"

"We'd like to know what happened. Is there someplace where we can talk?"

Marti led them to the room where the choir dressed. Two sets of robes, one red and one white with purple trim, hung along the walls. One wall was mirrored. A portable sewing machine and two ironing boards were set up.

"I'm Detective MacAlister."

The taller of the two extended his hand first. "Duncan Hamilton, and this is my brother Morgan. I'm the youngest, fifty-three. Henry was the oldest. We just did have enough time to fly here from Alabama." His native accent seemed to blend with some other influence, perhaps due to time spent away from the South.

"You know the cause of death?" Marti asked.

"Suffocation. With a pillow. Denise told us. But we can't get a copy of the autopsy report or the death certificate."

"The inquest hasn't been held yet. They won't be released until then."

Morgan, the shorter of the two, spoke. "And you don't know who did it yet?"

"No. It might help if you told me about Henry."

"We didn't see much of Henry once he joined the army," Duncan said. His accent was stronger.

"He wasn't much for writing, either," Morgan

said. "He let us know when he changed duty stations, but that was about it. He never went anyplace interesting. He got an honorable discharge, almost made it to retirement."

Marti recalled something about the best soldiers getting top assignments and mediocre soldiers filling in the other billets. Right now, there was no reason to check into Hamilton's military background.

"When did you meet Gladys?" she asked.

"At Momma's funeral, fifteen years ago," Duncan said. "We never did get a wedding invitation, just a Christmas card that year saying they were married. Didn't meet his daughters until today. Of course, he never saw my four kids either. The rest of us stayed close, but Henry always did keep to himself. We're not close in age."

"Henry was twelve years old when I was born; he'd joined the army when I was starting school," Morgan said. "I'm sorry we can't be of more help, but we didn't even know that he'd been in poor health."

"I don't think either of us will be able to come back for the inquest," Duncan said. "We run a business back home, can't stay away for any length of time. You will let us know what happens, and call if there's anything we can do to help?" He gave her his business card.

When Marti joined Vik he was having another

piece of sweet potato pie. "Belle just arrived, without the little man."

Marti looked where he nodded. Belle swayed as she hovered over Terri.

"You feeling really bad, ain't you, little sister? God, I'm sorry about that."

Terri sniffled but didn't answer.

"Got your belly full again and Daddy ain't even gonna be here to see the little one. Such a shame."

Tears trickled down Terri's face. The room became quiet, despite the gentleness in Belle's voice. Everyone seemed tense.

"Damned shame, him up and leaving you like this. I really am sorry, Terri, I truly am," Belle said. "You've got good old Ezra, though. Close your eyes and it must be almost like having Daddy."

Denise reached Belle's side and spoke so quietly that Marti didn't think anyone but Belle could have heard. Belle nodded, and Denise led her away.

"Where's Momma?"

Belle went to Gladys and put her arms about her shoulders, speaking in a much quieter tone. Marti angled her way to the buffet, getting close enough to eavesdrop.

". . . to use your insurance for this, Momma. Old Ezra can pick up the tab."

"We can talk about finances later."

"Old Ezra will be glad to help out," Belle said. "You're family. He's got a young, pretty wife to keep his old bones warm. And I know Daddy didn't leave you nothing much."

"Shush," Gladys insisted. "Get something to eat. You've had too much to drink."

"Oh Momma, I'm so sorry. I don't mean to embarrass you all the time, but I always seem to."

"Go eat," Gladys insisted.

To Marti's surprise, Belle complied.

Turning to Denise, Gladys said something in Gullah.

All Marti could make out was bits and pieces.

" 'Ceitful t'ing." Deceitful thing. "Day clean." That meant daybreak. Were they talking about when he died?

"Whymekso." Why was it so. Now something about hats again.

"Suppin' mek fuh enough." That was enough. Or, something was plenty. What were they talking about?

Belle stood next to Marti. "You trying to figure out that gibberish? I can't make no sense of it." She kicked off her shoes before filling her plate. "They haven't moved the john, have they?"

Marti shook her head. "Not that I know of."

"Good. I sure don't want any food, but Momma insisted. I'll probably have to puke time I'm through."

People cleared a path for her as she went over to Ezra with a loaded plate.

"Ezra, this funeral is free, ain't it? I mean, we are family. You ain't charging Momma nothing for this."

Ezra put his finger to his mouth.

"After all," Belle continued, "it isn't like Momma's got this big insurance policy to see her through." She winked at him.

Ezra smiled and patted her arm. "Your mother will want for nothing," he said. "And that's a promise."

"My God, Ezra," Belle said loudly. "You're a saint. Ain't there something in the Bible about looking after widows? It sure makes me feel better just knowing Momma's got you now. You got them old-fashioned values us young people don't have no more. Like I always tell everyone, Terri's got herself one damned decent old man."

"My daddy," Terri said, as if hearing her name was some kind of cue. "My daddy, my daddy." She began sobbing in earnest. One church sister brought Kleenex while another sat with her, rubbing her shoulders.

As Belle tried to offer Ezra a chicken leg the contents of her plate fell to the floor. Six women rushed over to clean up the mess. Belle turned to Gladys.

"I am so sorry, Momma. So sorry." Her mascara ran as she cried. "Oh shit," she said, suddenly rushing to the bathroom with her hand to her mouth.

Marti scanned the room for Denise and saw her standing in a corner by herself. As she watched, Denise pressed her fingertips to her temples as if her head hurt. Denise almost sagged as she leaned against the wall.

C H A P T E R

12

After Belle rushed to the bathroom, Denise followed. It was Denise who threw up.

"Denise! Are you all right?" Belle shook her. "You have to be all right."

"Stop, Belle. Stop it. I'm fine. It's just something I ate."

Denise turned away and went to the sink. "Just leave me alone for a few minutes, okay?"

"No, no, I can't. You're sick. I'll get Momma."

"Belle!" Denise shouted. "I'm fine. Just leave me alone. Go!"

The door closed as she splashed water on her face. Calmer, she went to the rear stairwell and made her way through the vestry to the church. The multicolored stained-glass window was illuminated by the recessed lighting along the walls. She saw Jesus, alone in the Garden, with ruby drops of blood on his forehead.

Denise sat in one of the pews, hugging herself and rocking. When she was a child she had come to this church and prayed that God would strike him dead and let him burn in hell. And now he was dead. Murdered. Her stomach lurched again. She tasted bile.

Now they would come, MacAlister and Jessenovik, asking questions. How could she tell them? What would she say? She had to tell them what he had done, but how could she? It would give all of them a motive for killing him. What was she going to do?

She had already lied to MacAlister about not going there the night he died. Now one lie would compound another. How could she explain it? What could she say that anyone would believe?

Soon she would have to lie about what a good husband and father he was, how much they loved him. She would have to, to protect everyone. What would happen to Belle if she had to answer questions about what he had done to her? What would happen to Momma if she ever found out? It was so easy to counsel others to confront and report abuse. But this had happened so long ago, when things like that weren't spoken of.

Denise could feel her heart pounding. She took a few deep breaths, tried to decide what she was going to do. How much longer could she lie to them and live with herself? What would happen to them if they told the truth? After all the damage he had already done, one of them would be accused of his murder. Premeditated murder.

She looked at the stained-glass Jesus. She had stopped praying for herself years ago and stopped believing that praying for anyone else would do any good. She just asked those who believed to pray for her and for the young people she worked with. She had no prayers to say now. She would wait.

If anyone found out that she had lied, she would lose credibility. She would lose her job. And all because of him. Because of him. Denise put her arms on the pew in front of her and put her head down.

"Sister Stevens."

She sat up, wiped her eyes.

The Reverend Douglas sat down beside her. "How you doing? Belle said she thought you were upset. I think you might be tired, too. Would you like to spend the night with us? Sister Esther would be glad to have you."

Such a nice man, just like his father. "I'm all right. It's just . . . there's so much to do."

He nodded. "And we're here to help whenever you need us. You know that. Let's just sit for a few minutes. Your family will be just fine."

She felt like leaning against him. She wished she could just tell him everything, but there was too much involved. Besides, she could never say any of it aloud.

As Denise made her way back to the social hall, she saw Marti coming out of the lavatory. For a moment, Denise wanted to run. Marti came toward her.

"Can we talk for a minute, Denise?"

"Sure."

"You look tired. I'm sorry to intrude, but we've placed your car near your parents' home within the time that your stepfather died."

Her car? It had been parked around the corner. All of the houses were dark. It had been so late. Who could have seen her? "What? My car?" She felt light-headed and leaned against the wall.

"Are you all right? Would you like to sit down somewhere?"

"No. Too much to do. No. I . . ."

She squeezed her eyes shut for a moment. She did not want to lie to this woman. She liked Marti. She had hoped that someday they could be friends. She took a deep breath, looked at Marti, and said, "I wasn't there." She hated the lie, hated everything that made it necessary. But somehow they all had to survive this.

"Where were you between two-thirty and three-thirty Saturday morning?"

"I was sleeping. I was home."

"Alone?"

"Yes. Alone."

Marti didn't believe her. She could hear it in her voice, see it in her eyes: How much could Marti prove? Had the person who had seen the car seen her too? There had to be some way out of this.

"Denise, please let me help you."

She had to think, but she was so tired. She needed time.

"Denise, I know this is your family, and I know how complicated that can make things, but I need to know the truth, I really do."

"I know."

"Tell me."

"I didn't kill him. I wasn't there."

"Did you want him dead?"

Denise shook her head. She hadn't always wanted him dead. For a while she had just wanted him to be her daddy. "We had to take him to the emergency room about a month ago," she said. "When we got back, Momma wanted to go to evening service, so I stayed with him. He wanted apple juice and I told him there was none, when there was, and brought him water." She had thought of that tonight, looking at him in the casket. Despite all he had done, she was sorry.

"Denise, please." Marti put her hand on Denise's shoulder. Denise wanted to believe this was just her "good cop" act.

"What did he deprive you of that made you retaliate in that way?"

"I can't tell you."

"You're going to have to. I'm going to investigate this case very thoroughly, and I will do nothing in haste. But I will find out who killed him. And why."

"I know," Denise said. "I know."

C H A P T E R
13

As Marti and Vik drove to see Deacon Franklin Tuesday afternoon, Marti thought about the funeral that morning. It was a gray day. It had been a somber gathering. Gladys wept quietly. Terri was subdued. Denise seemed withdrawn, hardly speaking to anyone and impassive until Belle sang "Precious Lord" a cappella. By the second verse, tears were streaming down Denise's face. Belle was crying too, but her voice never wavered. She had the truest, clearest soprano that Marti had ever heard. She and Vik listened in amazement.

The Reverend Douglas's message was stern; his text was titled "We Know Not the Day Nor the Hour." He referred to the deceased, but spoke to the living.

"We don't any of us have enough time left to delay getting right with the Lord. God knows.

He knows. Your actions. Your intentions. Your deepest secrets and innermost desires. God knows the heart. Don't justify your transgressions. Don't minimize your sins. Don't fool yourself into thinking God doesn't know, or has forgotten or just doesn't care.

"There's someone out there today who thinks he can come here and pretend to be right before God. There's someone out there today who thinks that because he can fool me, or fool you, he can fool the Lord. Do you not know that this night—this night—your soul could be demanded of you?

"Where are you going? Think on that. Where did Henry Hamilton go? Henry wasn't planning to leave us last Friday night. The last thing he said to me was, 'Reverend, see you at church Sunday.' Henry was not planning to leave here. Henry thought he had time. But that night, his soul was demanded of him. That night, he stood before God. If you think you've got all the time in the world to get right with God, think again. All the time in the world could end tonight."

As Marti left the church with Vik, she thought about her conversation with Denise the night before. Water instead of apple juice. She had never heard such pain expressed in such a trivial confession.

The Franklins lived near the municipal airport. Additions to the one-story house made it seem to sprawl across one corner of an acre lot. Tall pines with long, overhanging branches were evenly spaced along the length of the sidewalk and driveway. A sign on the front door directed them to a winterized porch in the rear, where nothing obstructed the view of the 6,000-foot runway and the control tower. A nice view on a sunny day, but it was overcast today.

The deacon and his wife were playing cards on a table set up near a fireplace with gas heat and fake logs.

"You two make yourself right at home. It's always good to see you, Sister MacAlister. Nice meeting you, Detective Jessenovik," the elderly deacon said. Franklin walked as if he was favoring his right knee. "Wonderful service this morning, wasn't it? We sent Henry off right proper. It sure brought back memories, hearing Belle sing."

"That girl still has such a fine voice," Mrs. Franklin agreed. "I keep praying she'll get her life turned around."

When Marti and Vik had settled on a sofa near the fireplace, Mrs. Franklin made her way over to the card table with the help of a walker. "Nice of you to visit, even if this is official business. I don't get out like I used to, so it's always good to have a little company every once in a while." The muscles on the left side of her face were not as strong as those on the right and there was a slight tremor in her voice.

Two chairs had been placed by the window, and binoculars were set up on stands for airplane watching.

Mrs. Franklin followed Marti's gaze. "We just watched another Challenger take off not ten minutes ago."

"A corporate jet?" Marti guessed.

"Why, yes. And a King Air came in right after lunch. That's a twin-engine," Mrs. Franklin explained.

Marti wouldn't consider getting into anything smaller than a 727, but she didn't say so.

The deacon brought glasses of cider. "I think I'd better tell you right off that Henry and I worked together for almost forty years, but we weren't close friends."

"Henry wasn't close to nobody. I don't even think he was close to his wife," Mrs. Franklin said. "I was surprised last night to see that he had family."

"Speak with charity," her husband reminded her.

"I'm too old for that. I'll just speak the truth, same as always."

"Is there any particular reason why you weren't close friends?" Marti asked.

"Most likely because Henry wanted it that

way," the deacon said. "He was like that with everyone."

"I always did think it was kind of strange myself," said Mrs. Franklin. "The man just shows up one Sunday, wearing his army uniform. He just joins the church right out of the blue."

"Now, Naomi. You've always been critical of Henry. Look at all he's done for the church."

"All of you did it, with the old Reverend Douglas. It wasn't the work of one man."

The deacon turned to Marti and Vik. "It was a real blessing, him coming when he did. We were ready to start a new church. Henry was a genius with the bookkeeping. We got us a beautiful church, and no debt, and we owe him a lot for that."

Mrs. Franklin patted his thigh. "My Eddie built this house. Him and Moses Gilmore know about all there is to know about construction. Henry Hamilton always got too much credit just because he took care of the finances and we ain't never had no problems with money. We ain't never had no problems with that building, either, and that's because of Eddie and Deacon Gilmore."

"The rest of us couldn't have done what Henry did, Naomi, not even the reverend."

"But the rest of you did it for free. You and Moses donated your time, and often as not, most of your materials. Henry's the only one who ended up getting a paycheck."

"And he's earned it, over the years."

"Oh, Eddie, you've always got to think the best about people. The man never said where he came from, where he'd been while he was in the service, or why he left the military with just three years to go until he retired. He never said nothing about himself at all. One day he was just here. And with all those pretty young women setting their sights on him, he ends up marrying Gladys. And it was quite a while before Terri came along. You'd think a man would want to start a family of his own, not have one ready-made. Not that I wasn't happy for poor Gladys."

Deacon Franklin chuckled. "If she ever hears you calling her 'poor Gladys,' you're going to get your comeuppance."

Mrs. Franklin shook her head. "No. That temper of hers is long gone. I always did like Gladys better before she got married. She was downright sassy. Belle and Denise behaved like little ladies then. None of that nonsense that Belle got away with later. The old Gladys wouldn't have tolerated it." She was silent for a moment. "I always did think Gladys let Belle get away with that outrageous behavior because she couldn't behave that way anymore." She laughed. "Remember the time Belle marched in with the choir and her slip was falling below her robe, and it kept getting lower and lower and she just kept marching and stepped out of it? We were probably lucky it wasn't her underpants."

Deacon Franklin laughed too.

"What what kind of a person was Henry?" Marti asked. Vik gave her a thumbs-up for being able to get a word in.

"Churlish," Mrs. Franklin said. "Him and Moses Gilmore couldn't agree on anything from the time they got that church built until we put on that addition."

"And they've gotten along just fine ever since, Naomi."

"Hah! And self-righteous. Real quick to see the speck in someone else's eye and miss the beam in his own. And he always had to have things his way."

"Now, Naomi. There was just that one time, when he didn't want that contractor to install the windows."

"No, there were all of those times when we wanted local folk getting the church's business and he insisted on bringing people in from out of town."

"Contractors here charge too much," Deacon Franklin said. "We can always get work done cheaper by folks who aren't from around here."

"Takes money out of our community, Eddie. Keeps our men out of work."

"Can't be helped."

"Other than being churlish . . ." Marti prompted.

"Quiet is a better word," Deacon Franklin said. "And solitary. Don't pay too much attention to Naomi. Henry was a good man. He just kept to himself."

Marti drove away slowly, her mood as gray as the day.

"I'm not pleased with that interview, Vik. The Franklins might have said more if we spoke with them separately."

What they did say had created subtle changes in her impressions of Henry Hamilton. The lack of close friendships was augmented by silence about his past. Marti had the feeling that Mrs. Franklin was telling her more than she seemed to be. Why had Henry married Gladys? Maybe she should see what she could find out about his time in the army. If everyone knew as little as the Franklins and Reverend Douglas did, this could be a tough case to solve.

When they returned to the precinct, Vik quickly scanned the reports that had come in while they were gone. "We got a make on three sets of prints found at the Hamilton residence. John Goodman, bigamist; Louie George, purse snatcher; Danzel Whittaker, con artist."

"Whittaker?"

"One of Ezra's cousin's kids."

"Where were his prints?"

"On the inner rim of the window in Hamilton's room. Report says that with existing conditions they could have been there a max of forty-eight hours."

Danzel was picked up at his girlfriend's house. Nice lady, according to the officer who brought him in. Forty at least, but real nice.

They interviewed the others first. John Goodman, a sales rep for a hospital supply company, had been in California from Wednesday until Saturday afternoon. Louie George was a plumber's apprentice. He had unclogged a drain in the Hamiltons' bathroom Thursday morning and helped Henry take out a few bags of trash. Gladys hadn't been home while he was there.

Danzel was circling the table when Marti and Vik walked into the interview room. Vik entered first.

"I haven't done anything," he said. He noticed Marti and smiled.

He must have a thing for older women, Marti decided, and smiled back. He was tall and slender, light-skinned, and wore his hair in a curly perm. He gave her his profile, then a full face with another smile. Full of himself, Momma would say, Marti thought.

"Sit," Vik ordered.

When Danzel looked at her, she shrugged and

he sat down. Vik straddled a chair. Marti leaned against the wall, arms folded.

"Are you sure you don't want a lawyer present?" Vik asked.

"For what? I haven't done anything."

Marti had stopped being surprised by this. In Chicago, an attorney was the first thing they asked for.

"Where were you Friday night, Danzel?" Vik asked.

"With my lady. Why would I be anywhere else?"

"When's the last time you were at the Hamiltons'?"

"Not Friday night. Ask the lady. Besides, I work for Ezra. Why shouldn't I go there?"

"Think, Whittaker. When were you there?"

"Ma'am," he appealed to Marti, "I haven't done anything, honest. I don't understand what he's asking. I was with my lady."

Before Marti could answer, Vik stood up and leaned over the table. His wiry eyebrows almost came together as he spoke. "The last time you were there."

"Tuesday, I think. No, maybe it was Wednesday or Thursday. I . . . um . . . I checked a window. It was stuck."

"Who asked you to?"

"The old man."

Vik turned and walked out of the room. Marti

gave Danzel what she hoped seemed to be a sympathetic look, and followed. Outside, Vik said. "Let's call Gladys."

When he hung up the phone he seemed puzzled. "She's not sure what day it was, but she says Henry mentioned having Danzel come over last week. She wasn't sure why, either."

"Vague, isn't she?"

"Lying, MacAlister. I'm sure she's lying. But why? We'll have to let him go."

"Have we got anything else?" she asked.

"Of course not. Those who were there that night are coming in to be printed much sooner than I thought they would. Serves them right, disturbing a scene of a crime." He rubbed his hands together, pleased.

"Too bad we didn't need a sample of Danzel's pubic hair," Marti said. "That really would have inconvenienced him."

"I don't believe you said that, MacAlister." He almost smiled.

C H A P T E R
14

It was getting dark by the time Marti arrived at Deacon Gilmore's. He owned three red-brick two-story buildings on the south side of town, and lived in the one on the corner. She had to climb a flight of stairs to get to the front door. The sloping land from porch to sidewalk had been stripped of grass. There was no bell, and the front door wasn't locked. Inside, the hallway was well lit. The mailbox indicated that Gilmore lived in the second-floor apartment. The varnish had been worn off the center of the stairs and the swirled plaster patterns on the wall were water-stained and chipped.

"Sister MacAlister, I'm so sorry that such a sad occasion brings you here. So nice of you to attend Henry's service this morning. Reverend Douglas sure did tell the truth. Henry would have been pleased with that sermon. And Belle—that liquor hasn't harmed her voice at all."

Marti stepped into a spacious, well-kept living room with a large window that looked out on Lake Michigan. A stereo system took up an entire wall.

"Let me get you something. Coke? Coffee?"

She didn't want anything, but thought he would be offended if she refused his hospitality. "Coke will be fine."

Marti sat in one of two easy chairs by the window. She could see the cemetery a few blocks away, and beyond it, the placid, gray-blue waters of the lake.

"Restful, isn't it?" Deacon Gilmore said, returning with a tall glass of ice and a can of soda. "The neighborhood is going from bad to worse, but this window will keep me here 'til the Lord takes me or they tear the place down."

There was talk of this area being leveled and replaced by a freeway.

Gilmore was a small, pot-bellied man, five-seven maybe, very dark, and bald. She guessed his age at about sixty-five. Her mother would have called him a "musty old man" because of his odor, not strong, but lingering. Marti thought of it as the smell of old things—old paper, clothes, and furniture, and places that had gone too long without fresh air.

"I'm honored that you've come, sister, but I'm not sure I can be of much help."

Such a gentleman, Marti thought. "You worked with Deacon Hamilton for years, helped found Mount Gethsemane."

"We split off from Mount Tabor," Gilmore said. "The old Reverend Douglas was such a fine young preacher back then. It's hard to think of him dead, even after seventeen years. He came to Mount Tabor as an assistant. And he had a lot of good ideas about going into the community and reaching out to people. Folks at Mount Tabor didn't want that." He chuckled. "Now there is no Mount Tabor."

"What exactly did you and Deacon Hamilton do?"

"Well, Henry was a military man. He had more schooling than the rest of us, and knew a lot about buying things and keeping records and handling finances. The old reverend knew how to raise money. I'm a carpenter by trade. I can fix all kinds of things, make all kinds of things, too. Me and Eddie Franklin had been repairing things at Mount Tabor for years. We all took what expertise we had and put our heads together and built a church. Fine building too, isn't it? Brick. Solid. And real workmanship. You see how everything around the altar is hand-carved? I did that myself. And that stained-glass picture window of Jesus in the Garden of Gethsemane—we had that made special. Nothing but the best, all of it."

"And you served on the deacons' board together?"

Gilmore gave her an appraising look before answering. "For a number of years we didn't agree on most things. Then we got older, and now one of us is gone. He was at last week's board meeting. He looked poorly, but I sure didn't think I'd never see him again. I wasn't feeling so good myself, ended up going to the hospital Friday night."

That would save her the trouble of asking him where he was.

"You and Henry went back a long way. Did he have any enemies?"

"None that I know of. I'd imagine Joe Nathan Watkins was a little unhappy when Henry married Gladys, but other than that . . ."

No friends. No enemies. Just Gladys. Why her? Why would a conservative, taciturn man like Henry marry a woman whose morals, in those days, would have been considered loose, to say the least?

"So you knew Henry when he was courting Gladys?"

Gilmore rubbed his chin, then stroked his thigh before answering. "Gladys was a good woman, no matter what anyone said. She stayed in the church despite having those children, worked to support them and herself right up until she got married. She's still a fine-looking woman, too."

Watching the lake was soothing. Marti resisted the urge to close her eyes for a minute. "Did they have a long courtship?"

"A few months, maybe. There was talk that he might be seeing her, but things were kept kind of quiet. I went to Arkansas for a couple of weeks. When I came back, they were married. It sure surprised me. But then, Henry always was kind to widows with children, and concerned about single mothers. I always thought it was something personal in his life that made that so important to him. And now he's been smothered. Sounds like something a woman would do, doesn't it?" He shook his head. "You never know what's gonna happen in this life. You just never know."

"What was Gladys like in those days?"

His face took on a brooding expression as he looked out the window. "Gladys was something else. Pretty. Real pretty. And alive, so alive. Back then, Gladys seemed to be a lot like Denise is now. But she was really just as wild as Belle."

He thought for a moment. "A lot of men would have jumped at the chance to marry Gladys, even though she had those little girls. We thought she only had eyes for Joe Nathan

Watkins. It was a surprise to all of us when she married Henry."

"Who was Joe Nathan? Denise and Belle's father?"

"Why, yes." He seemed surprised that she didn't know.

"Why do you think she married Henry and not him?"

He rubbed his thigh. "Couldn't. Joe Nathan was already married. There was never no talk about him getting a divorce, neither. Talk was that it was Gladys who chased after him. When she married Henry, most folks thought she must be in the family way again. That could have been what she told him. I always did wonder if she tricked old Henry."

Marti sipped her Coke. Enough ice had melted to dilute it. "Was Henry that easy to trick?"

"Not unless there was something in it for him."

"And what might that be?"

"I never could figure that out. I always wondered if he didn't trick her, too. I never knew Henry to get the worse end of a deal. That would be something, wouldn't it, if they both tricked each other."

As evening approached, the lake became more difficult to discern. The room was getting dark, but Gilmore didn't turn on a light. Marti tried not to relax. She didn't want to get drowsy. Shifting in the chair, she sat straighter.

"Did you ever marry?"

"Me? No. I was never inclined to. I like looking after myself."

"Did Gladys change after she married?"

"It was like someone had poured water on a fire." He seemed saddened by that.

"What about Henry?"

"I can't imagine Henry ever changing. Henry was a lot smarter than the rest of us. He always knew what he wanted and how to get it. It's hard to imagine him dead."

Gilmore looked around the room. "I hardly notice the dark sometimes." He switched on a light. "Henry was smart in a lot of ways that most folks didn't give him credit for. He was smart about people and could read them like books. He wasn't as sharp or as fast near the end, but that's because he was sickly. Quiet, he was. Too quiet, some said. But sometimes quiet folks are watching you. And old Henry always was."

Gilmore collected the glass and the pop can. He seemed self-conscious, as if he had said too much.

Marti drove back to the precinct to write her reports. Instead of going home afterward, she went to see her friend Ben Walker. It was getting late, and everyone at her house would be in bed or getting ready for bed. The house would be too quiet. Her room, functional, not cozy, would seem barren. Her bed, single now, not king-size, would be empty. She wasn't sleepy yet, and she didn't want to be alone right now, the way Deacon Gilmore was. There was a light on when she pulled up in front of Ben's house, so she rang the bell.

Ben was taller than she was, a large man, but muscular, not fat. He was a paramedic, and on those occasions when she had seen him at work, she had seen a sensitive, compassionate man who calmed people and put them at ease. He smiled when he saw her.

"Just passing by," she said. "Again."

She had done this a couple of weeks ago when she couldn't go home. They went to the den. Ben was watching the Bulls game. He turned down the volume.

"Beer?"

"Sure. Just one. Then I've got to go."

Ben sat beside her. He didn't ask any questions. He didn't make any demands. He was a widower with a son the same age as Marti's. He understood.

The room was small, crowded with a TV, sofa, and chair. There was a jumble of newspapers and magazines and mail on the rolltop desk, the clutter of children's games on the floor. On a card table set up in one corner, a large jigsaw puzzle was partially completed. She had helped with a few pieces the last time she was here.

"I'm kind of wired tonight," she said. "If I go home I won't be able to sleep."

"And your place will be too quiet. Like mine. It gets hard sometimes, after Mike goes to bed, trying to figure out what to do with myself."

"Even after all this time?" His first wife had died in a car accident five years ago.

"Well, for the first couple of years I didn't deal with any of it. I chased every woman over eighteen and under forty-five who wasn't in a wheelchair and could talk and chew gum at the same time. And I was willing to relax those standards."

Marti had heard from friends that Ben wasn't dating anyone now because his son had begun having problems in school. She didn't ask.

"When I remarried it was another escape from reality," he said.

He was divorced now from his second wife.

"You're handling Johnny's death, Marti. You're there for your kids, you're doing your job. You're looking out for everyone but yourself, but at least that keeps you busy. You don't waste time feeling sorry for yourself and being angry because things aren't the way you want them to be. You're doing a lot better than I did."

And then there were nights like tonight, when she ran out of things to do and still had too much energy to go to sleep, and she was alone in ways that only Johnny could change. "This isn't how it was supposed to be, not for either of us."

"Carol was pregnant when she died," Ben said.

"I didn't know that."

"Nobody knows that. She had just told me."

Marti wanted to say "I'm sorry," but so many people had said that to her that she knew how empty it sounded. "You wanted the baby."

"I wanted *her*. I wanted my life back." He got up, came back in a few minutes with another beer. "Sometimes I still get angry."

"At who?"

"At her, for not seeing the truck, for not being able to avoid it. At myself for blaming her for skidding on an icy road. At myself for not being home that day to go to the store for her. At myself, for still being alive. At myself."

There was a weariness in his voice that Marti had never heard before.

"I still want that day back, even after all this time. You have to watch out for the 'if only's and 'what if's, Marti. Some nights they can really kick butt." He gulped down the beer. "And you have to watch out for this stuff, too. My absolute limit is three cans."

When the game was over, the ten o'clock news came on half an hour late.

"I've got to be going," Marti said.

"Tired now?"

"No, but I need to iron some blouses."

"You had to go to that funeral this morning, didn't you?"

"Things like that shouldn't bother me anymore."

Ben looked at her. There was sadness in his eyes. "I knew Carol most of my life. We grew up on the same street, went to the same schools. I resent it when someone tells me I should have gotten over it by now. I think you get used to it, I think you go on with your life. But I can see Carol as clearly right now as I could the morning she died."

Marti nodded. "I know."

She finished the beer, put the empty can on the table. "I've got to go. But I'm glad I stopped by."

She looked down at her hand. She still hadn't taken off her wedding band, just switched it to her right hand because she was a widow. "Are we . . . becoming friends just because we're alone?"

"Maybe."

"I don't know where I'm at," she admitted. "And with the hours I've been putting in lately I'm too tired to figure it out." She stood up. "I've got to go home now and get some sleep."

Ben put his arm about her shoulders as he walked her to the door. She turned to him before she left.

"Thanks."

"For what?"

"Not taking advantage."

He pulled her against him for a moment. She leaned into his chest, inhaled the light scent of his cologne. Reaching up, she touched a stubble of beard. When they kissed it was slow and gentle.

C H A P T E R
15

On Wednesday morning, Marti went to Whittaker's Funeral Home. She hoped Terri would be calm enough by now to speak in complete sentences without interspersing them with "my daddy." It was a spacious house with living quarters on the second floor. Marti wasn't superstitious, and she knew the dead couldn't harm you, but she couldn't imagine cooking and eating and playing in such close proximity to the dead. It seemed a little like living at the morgue.

An elderly woman opened the door and introduced herself as Mrs. Whittaker, Senior. Walking briskly, she led Marti upstairs. The maroon velvet curtains were drawn and the long, wide hallway was dark until Mrs. Whittaker flicked a switch and three chandeliers came on. Curious, Marti looked about as they went to the rear of the house. The carpet, also maroon, was thick enough to prevent their footsteps from being heard below. Marti felt like she was walking through a museum. The Victorian chairs and settees had plastic-covered seats. Plastic covered the lace and linen doilies on the sideboards and tables. Vinyl runners protected heavily traveled areas of carpet.

Terri was in a small sitting room. No plastic here, except for the carpet runners. The sofa and chair as well as the recliner Terri was resting on were gray leather, and the tables had matching inlays. A little girl sat on the floor quietly assembling a puzzle. The child was a miniature version of Terri. An ugly newborn doll lay sprawled in the corner. A sensible child, Marti decided, if she was smart enough not to play with it.

Terri seemed listless. She looked at Marti but didn't speak. Marti sat on the couch without being invited.

"How are you feeling?" she asked, not really wanting to know.

Terri patted her stomach. "It's a boy. I saw it on the ultrasound." She sounded exhausted. "I'm naming him Henry Ezra. Poor Daddy, he won't be here to see him. He had cancer, you know. I took him to Miss Kazzie. She would have healed him if there had been enough time."

"A faith healer?" Marti asked.

"Yes. She said she could see a dark shadow hovering over him. It must have been whoever put that pillow on his face and held it there until he stopped breathing. Poor Daddy. Do you know who did it?"

"Not yet." Marti felt as if she were speaking to a child.

"You don't have any idea who it was?"

"No."

"Maybe you never will."

"That happens."

That answer seemed to please Terri. "Was Daddy awake when they did it? If he was sleeping he might not have known, but if he was awake would it hurt?"

"I would assume so."

"It must hurt when you're trying to breathe but you can't. Ezra knows but he won't tell me. He says I shouldn't talk about things like that. Does it take a long time to die?"

Maybe living in a funeral home was enough to make you a little odd, Marti thought. But then, all of Gladys's daughters were different, even Denise. What was it about Henry? What had he done to these women?

"Is this your daughter?" Marti asked.

"Yes, that's Zaar." Her voice was stern.

Zaar stopped playing. Immobile, she watched her mother.

"How old are you, Zaar?" Marti asked. Such an odd name, she thought.

The little girl hesitated, looked at Terri, then held up four fingers. She was tiny for four.

"Four and a half." Terri said. "Say it. Four and a half."

The child shrank back against the wall as she whispered the words.

"That's better," Terri said. "And don't you dare sit there and wet your pants again today."

Zaar nodded.

Terri shifted in the chair, turning toward Marti. Zaar picked up a puzzle piece.

"Where were you the night your father died?" Marti asked. Terri's attitude toward her daughter disturbed her. She wondered if Denise was aware of it. She had not got the impression that Terri and Denise were close.

"Last Friday?" Terri said. "I was right where I always am. I hardly ever go out anymore." She leaned toward Marti. "Men," she said in a low voice. "They can't stay away from me. Not even when I'm like this. One followed me home yesterday."

Marti thought she must be joking. Then she wondered if Danzel was one of those men.

After Marti left, Terri wondered why she had come. It couldn't be because of Danzel. He didn't have anything to do with Daddy dying. He told her that. He promised. He loved her and he knew how much she loved Daddy. She did love Daddy. She did.

She needed Danzel here to protect her. What if one of the men who kept following her home came into the house? God, why couldn't they leave her alone? She used to be safe when she was pregnant. This time it didn't stop them. They whispered to her when she walked by them in the store. They stared at her in church. She couldn't go anywhere anymore. It had been like this for as long as she could remember. What was wrong with her? Even Daddy couldn't leave her alone.

Poor Daddy. He had wanted to go to the doctor, but she couldn't let him. The doctors would have killed him. They would have cut his stomach open and let air in and then the cancer would have spread real fast and he would have died. She'd convinced him that Miss Kazzie could help. Even when the tumors kept getting bigger, she had taken him back.

When he called the doctor and made that appointment, she didn't know what else to do, so she told him she would tell Reverend Douglas about what they had done together when she was little. He had looked at her so strangely that day. Then he'd showed her the insurance policy. It was made out to the three of them, but she had made him change it because Belle and Denise didn't love him. Now it was all hers. She would have to call the insurance agency soon. She didn't need the money now, but he had wanted her to have it.

He had tried to sneak to the doctor again last month, but Momma told her about it, and when it was time to keep the appointment she was right there, at the house, watching him. She would have told Reverend Douglas, she would have, to keep Daddy alive, to keep Daddy from getting operated on and dying. She hadn't wanted him to die.

He had been sick for so long when he died. In the casket, he didn't look anything like himself. She had got up several times during the night to look at the snapshots Ezra had taken of him, and Daddy looked every bit as bad as she thought he did.

Zaar coughed.

"Shut up!" Terri said. She couldn't stand the sound of Zaar's whining, couldn't stand to hear her talk, couldn't stand to watch her play.

Ezra hadn't expected her to stay pregnant this long. That was why they were making Zaar stay with her. They thought she would lose this baby too, that then she might learn to love Zaar. She had heard them talking, Ezra and his mother. They thought that once she gave up on having a boy she would take better care of Zaar. But there was no need for her to care for Zaar.

Mother Whittaker was here, somewhere. Why didn't she come and get Zaar out of here?

What would have happened when Zaar turned five? Would Daddy have sent for her, too? If she had known she was carrying a girl she wouldn't have gone through with it.

She wanted to shout at Zaar to go away, but Mother Whittaker and Ezra would hear her. Instead, she picked up the doll's cradle and threw it across the room. Zaar began to cry. Terri closed her eyes and pretended to be asleep when Mother Whittaker came and took Zaar from the room.

C H A P T E R
16

When Marti arrived at the precinct after seeing Terri, she brought blueberry muffins that Joanna had baked before going to school. Slim and Cowboy, the two Vice cops who shared the office, were at their desks.

Slim, who was tall, tan, and flirtatious, gave her a dimpled, Cupid's-bow smile. He reeked of Obsession for Men.

"Hey. What's this?" He opened the container. "Way to go, Miss Marti."

Cowboy pushed back his five-gallon hat, revealing wavy blond hair. "What's this? Can that cute crime crusader from Chicago solve crimes, apprehend criminals, and make muffins too?"

Slim sniffed. "Smells good." He took a bite. "And definitely passes the 'my momma can bake these' test. I told you Big Mac could cook."

"Joanna made them," Marti said.

Slim shrugged. "So much for requesting some banana bread tomorrow morning." He reached for his coat. "We've got to head over to the courthouse. We've finally got the case of a lifetime. Limp Nick the Clown."

"Don't explain. Lady present," Vik warned.

"Come on, Jessenovik," Cowboy drawled. "You've been riding with MacAlister long enough to know she's a cop."

"Right," Slim agreed, ducking as Marti threw a pen at him. "This is the guy you've been reading about in the *News-Times*. He dresses up in his little clown suit, gets into his little rust-and blue van, and wags his little whatsee at little old ladies. And we nailed him. We'll be celebrities before this is over."

"You know, Slim," Marti said. "There's not a hell of a lot of difference between what you do and cleaning toilets."

Slim grinned. "I knew you'd be impressed. Wait until you see us on the six o'clock news."

After they left, Vik said, "Why did Gladys Hamilton lie about Danzel Whittaker?"

"Vik, that's the tenth time you've asked that."

He thought for a minute. "It's only the fourth time. I just can't figure it out. I hope it doesn't mean she's covering up for Denise. I'm still not satisfied that that old man was giving us reliable information about her license plate number."

"I think Gladys and Denise are both lying,"

143

Marti said. "I don't know what they're not telling us, or why, but they're not telling us the truth." The lying made their job that much harder.

"You think Denise was there that night?"

"When I talked with her, she lied."

"She's one of us, Marti."

"She's a suspect. She's also under a lot of stress. I think they all are. If one of them did it, I think it will be too much to live with." Questioning someone she worked with and respected during a homicide investigation was one of the few situations Marti hadn't dealt with while she was on the force in Chicago. Knowing Denise wasn't being honest was frustrating.

"If it was Gladys," Vik said, "she sure didn't do it for the money. She has a ten-thousand-dollar insurance policy, net of funeral expenses. There's no safety deposit box. The house is paid for, but she's going to have a hard time with him dead. His pension and Social Security will be cut."

"I wonder if she knew that. A lot of women have no idea what their death benefits are."

Vik took the last muffin and shared it with her. "Who's to say Belle didn't slip out of the motel that night? She could have been in a blackout. Or, it could have been a burglar. According to the evidence tech a six-year-old could have come in through the back door. I bet the perp didn't think we could prove suffocation. A lot of people think you can hold something over somebody's face and get away with it. We've got to wrap up these routine investigations and put more time in on this." He cleared his desk and began going through his in-basket. "Whoever it was, they could be in big trouble. We've got a victim who never got so much as a parking ticket. He's a veteran of the Korean Conflict, helped build a church, and made an honest woman of someone with loose morals who had two children out of wedlock. I'm sure a jury would have a lot of sympathy for whoever killed him."

"Maybe they would," Marti said. "I think Henry Hamilton was an abuser."

"Denise's stepfather? I don't believe it."

The more Marti thought about Terri, the more certain she became. "I don't know what kind of abuse or who was abused, but something went on in that house. When we find out, we might find out who did it."

"That would give us a motive," Vik agreed.

Marti scanned her list of people to be interviewed and passed it to Vik. "We've got to have some division of work here. There's too much to do, and we've got a real backlog of routine investigations. The time we've spent on this case has made it worse. You like paperwork and reports and I like talking with people."

Vik read the list. "Miss Hannah Hardy. How old is she?"

"About ninety."

"I thought so. Why don't you start on this list. I'll get going on the paperwork. We'll see where we are at the end of the day. I'd like to leave on time tonight. Mildred's feeling a little under the weather."

"Okay," Marti agreed. "I'm itching to meet this Joe Nathan Watkins, the guy Gladys had the hots for. I suppose I should talk with Vera Holmes, too, even though she just started helping Henry with the church books a few weeks ago." What she really needed was a good gossip, and she was hoping that Miss Hardy, the elderly lady that Reverend Douglas had mentioned, would provide it. Neither Marti nor Vik wanted to say it, but sometimes, when domestic issues were involved, women could be more effective. This seemed to be that kind of case.

Miss Hardy lived with her family in a brick ranch house three blocks from the high school. A hoop and backboard were attached to the garage and five teenage boys were shooting baskets when Marti pulled up. The high school had a half-day.

As she walked toward the front door the tallest boy greeted her. "Hi, Officer MacAlister." He shifted from one foot to the other then stuck out his hand. "Jeffrey Reed. Varsity basketball. I've seen you at Joanna's games. Tell her I said hi."

"Sure. Nice meeting you, Jeffrey."

Maybe Chris, the football player Joanna was dating, had a little competition. She didn't think dating just one boy was a good idea at Joanna's age, but Joanna hadn't been eager to date anyone a few months ago.

A tall, slender woman opened the door.

"Mrs. Hardy?"

"Yes, come right in. Aunt Hannah is waiting for you." She led Marti to the rear of the house. "She's my husband's great-aunt, ninety years old come Christmas. I told her about Mr. Hamilton. We don't like to spring too many surprises on her. Don't worry about tiring her. She loves company. Keeps her mind active. She'll talk about this for days."

Marti entered a corner room with wide windows on two sides. The curtains were pulled back and sunlight streamed in. Plants were stacked on a tiered stand in the corner and everything was yellow and lavender and Nile green. Miss Hardy sat in a rocker near a table by the window. Pillows were propped behind her and she had her feet up on a hassock. An old quilt covered her legs. From where she sat she could watch the boys playing basketball, or look up and down the street.

Miss Hardy looked her age. She had a scattering of liver spots on her tan face and the backs of her hands.

"Officer MacAlister." She smiled and suddenly seemed ten years younger. "It's a pleasure to meet you. I hear such good things about you."

"May I call you Miss Hannah?"

The old woman nodded.

"Thank you. It's good of you to see me on such short notice."

The niece pushed an easy chair closer and put up a tray table. "Coffee or tea, officer?"

"Coffee, please. Black," Marti said.

Miss Hannah studied her face for a moment. "You're the first colored female police officer I've ever seen close up. I wouldn't have even imagined coloreds being part of the police department when I was a girl. Interesting, how much everything has changed." She covered Marti's hand with her own and squeezed with more strength than Marti expected. "Good changes. Good for us all. Praise God, I've lived to see it."

Her niece wheeled in a cart, poured for her great-aunt, and gave Marti a steaming cup of coffee. "Just ring your bell if you need anything else, dear."

Miss Hannah fussed with her tea, something herbal like Joanna preferred. "You've come to talk about Gladys and Henry."

Marti nodded.

"The *News-Times* said he died of undetermined causes following a lengthy illness. It's not surprising somehow, Henry not having a heart attack or dying in his sleep. He was such a quiet man, sneak right up on you before you knew he was there. I never knew him to raise his voice, or speak harshly, or talk bad about anyone. But for all of that, he was one of them who could say a lot without ever opening his mouth. I didn't like him much, to be honest."

She looked out the window, then at Marti.

"It's hard to decide what to tell you. Is there anything special you want to know?"

"Whatever you can remember," Marti said.

Miss Hannah smiled. "She was Gladys Stevens when I met her. Proud people, the Stevenses. Society folks. Part of Gladys's family settled here in 1853. Her momma told that to everybody. They came here from the islands off the coast of South Carolina and say one of their ancestors was an Indian princess. Gladys's mother and some friends founded the first social club for colored women in Lincoln Prairie in 1924. They did little things like visiting shut-ins." She chuckled. "My mother always said they went wherever they could find a little gossip and then they sat around making quilts and talking about folks. To join, your family had to be here three generations." She paused, looking at Marti over the rim of her cup as she sipped her tea.

"The way I hear it, when Gladys came up pregnant with the first baby, her mother wanted her to go to their people in Charleston and have it there, give it up for adoption and tell everyone here she was in college. I've got to hand it to Gladys, though. She stayed here, held her head up, kept herself to herself, and kept both babies. She never did say who the daddy was, but both Denise and Annabelle are the spitting image of Joe Nathan Watkins. A poor fellow, Joe Nathan was then. Married he was, and married he stayed. His wife is dead now. I always did believe Gladys loved him. That was a lot for a woman to go through back then. The first baby might have been considered a mistake, but not two."

"How well did you know Gladys?"

"I didn't know any of them until I joined Mount Gethsemane back in the forties. I just knew about them. We was circus folk. My daddy trained horses. Momma and I were seamstresses." She fingered the quilt, frayed in places. "My mother made this. It still warms me." She didn't speak for a moment, then said, "My granddaddy settled here in the late eighteen hundreds. There used to be sulky races at the fairgrounds back then. He trained horses. Two of his brothers were harness drivers. The youngest was a janitor for the Besleys, worked at the brewery 'til they closed the place down. City's got a school built there now." She chuckled again. "Uncle Esmond used to bring us a bucket of the yeast they used and Momma would make the best buckwheat pancakes. Lord, I can almost taste them now, they was so good. None of us were society folks, though, nobody the likes of those Stevenses would ever want to know. Of course we kept up with those who were."

She sipped her tea.

"Henry Hamilton came here while Eisenhower was president. I have no idea of when, exactly. He was a soldier then, assigned to the army base. Joining the church was a smart thing for a man to do then, if he was looking for a woman. And he dated a number of them. He courted the widow Blake for a while, then Gladys seems to have caught his eye."

"Did the women he dated have anything in common?"

"Children. I always wondered if maybe he couldn't have any. But I guess that wasn't the case, since they had Terri. Of course, that did take them quite a while."

"Did the widow Blake have children?"

"Yes. Three, I think. I remember folks saying that was why they didn't marry, that he didn't want the responsibility. Then he up and married Gladys."

"Was it sudden? Or unexpected?"

"As I recall. He had courted Della Blake for a good while. Then he courts Gladys maybe two months and there's a wedding. Nothing big or fancy, just the immediate family. And she sure didn't wear white. Some folks said Gladys had learned to work root from her people in South Carolina and that's how she got Henry so fast, others said a girl with loose morals would do certain things to please a man when she laid with him that a lady would not."

"Do you think Gladys had loose morals?"

Miss Hannah thought about it. "I think Gladys loved Joe Nathan. I've got a strong feeling that she didn't love Henry quite the same way. Henry got her away from her mother. I think she did a lot of things to get her mother's attention, but having those babies wasn't one of her better ideas. Her mother tolerated her after they were born, but Gladys didn't get to go to none of the parties her sister Dolly did. She didn't have a big, fancy coming out at one of them cotillions like Dolly did. And she didn't go to teachers' college like Dolly, either. Gladys worked nights cleaning offices. She had to give her mother half her earnings and she had to take care of her own babies all day. Nobody was allowed to help her with them. Her mother was afraid she'd keep having babies if they did."

Miss Hannah rang a bell and the niece returned, bringing more hot water. She assisted her aunt to the bathroom and settled her back in her rocking chair. "I heard Gladys laughing once," she said. "I think it was during a revival. I remember thinking how I'd never heard her laugh since she'd gotten married. I've never heard her laugh again."

"Did Henry date anyone else that you know of?"

"He could have. Henry was a fine-looking man. He had job security, and even bought himself a house. A lot of those church sisters were upset when Gladys caught him." The old lady laughed. "There was talk every now and again that he was helping another widow or single woman. It could have been envy. Gladys sure hasn't been anything less than respectable since the wedding. She got real active in the church once she had that ring on her finger, and not just because her husband was a deacon. Those young matrons who became her friends once she had that wedding band on hadn't been none too friendly before."

"Was Joe Nathan the only other man that Gladys dated?"

"As far as I know. Gladys wasn't flirtatious. She was a pretty little thing and could have had her pick of most of the young men at church. I kind of think Moses Gilmore was sweet on her. He was a shy young man. Not near as handsome as Joe Nathan and Henry. How a man looks can be real important when you're as young as she was."

"Do you remember much about the girls, Belle and Denise?"

Miss Hannah chuckled. "Everybody remembers Belle. That child was a real hellion. Babies or not, Gladys was respectful to everyone and always carried herself like she'd been raised to. Denise was a good child, always obedient and helpful, and so quiet. Not Belle. That child walked right out of her drawers on Palm Sunday. If you want to know more about them when they were coming up, see Eloise DeVeaux and her sister Camille. They would have taught them in elementary school."

Miss Hannah adjusted the quilt. Her fingers lingered over several squares. "I know there's a reason why you're asking all this, and listening to an old woman rambling on, but I don't suppose you'll tell me what it is."

"Maybe later," Marti said. "If I can."

C H A P T E R
17

When Gladys tasted her soup it was cold. Had she sat here that long? She looked at the clock. It was almost three in the afternoon. She should get dressed, and yesterday's dishes were still in the sink. She couldn't remember the last time she'd vacuumed. There was so much to do. Denise would worry if she saw her like this. Bootsie meowed and rubbed against her legs. Had she remembered to feed her this morning?

"Are you hungry?" she asked, picking her up. Bootsie settled on her lap and began purring as Gladys stroked the fur between her ears. What was she going to do? Would there never be an end to worry?

Why had that detective called yesterday asking her about Ezra's kin, Danzel? She didn't know nothing about that boy. Henry didn't trust him. He had never allowed him in the house and sure wouldn't have let him in if he came here. When had she last seen Danzel? What kind of a question was that? Did this have something to do with Terri? She couldn't ask. She said Danzel had come here sometime last week because that had to be what the detective wanted to know, but then she couldn't say when or why, so she said she was out and Henry mentioned it to her.

The more she thought about it, the more she felt she should have told the truth. She was afraid to ask why they wanted to know. Maybe it was some kind of trick question. If they found out that Denise was the only one who came here the night Henry died, that she hadn't heard or seen anyone else, what would happen?

What did Ezra's kin have to do with anything? She couldn't ask Terri for fear of upsetting her. That girl couldn't keep herself away from a pretty man. Lord alone knew why she hadn't married one. She'd chosen Ezra, and she was going to have to respect him. Not that Terri had ever respected anyone. Not her parents. Not herself. Willful and spoiled, that was Terri. Her and Belle were both trifling. Denise was the only one with any sense. She had tried to raise them right. What had happened? If Henry had been more affectionate, if he had helped discipline them . . . She married him so they'd have a father, but except for watching them so she could go to church, he might as well not have been there at all.

Before they were married he would put Belle and Denise on his knee, buy them presents, take them for ice cream. Once they were married it was like they didn't exist anymore. He shut himself up in his room at night or went off to his church meetings and couldn't be bothered with any of them. That alone proved that what Della Blake had told her about Henry could not have been true. For a moment Gladys wondered what had become of Della. A while ago she had heard she was in poor health. Served Della right for telling her those terrible things about Henry because she was jealous. Henry couldn't have done anything that awful to her children. Surely, Denise would have told her if he did. Denise had made a good life for herself. Terri had married well. She was just spoiled and selfish. And Belle . . . well, two out of three wasn't bad.

Gladys stacked the dishes and filled the sink with hot, soapy water. She shouldn't have told Denise that Henry threw out her hats. Denise was already mad about Henry spitting on her Wednesday night. Telling her about the hats had made it worse.

Gladys began washing the glasses. If only she never had taken things into her own hands and made Henry get sick. She should have left everything to the Lord. Instead she had begun interfering, feeding Henry that pokeweed so he'd be too sick to pick at her, and nag, and complain. His condition, she said, so folks would think it was his heart. She didn't know what those lumps in his side were but she hinted at cancer. How she had enjoyed watching him fail. But now Denise was in danger. Dear Lord, what had she done?

If anything happened to Denise, she wouldn't have anyone. Wait until you have children, her momma had told her, saying it like it was some kind of curse. She had wanted a boy who looked just like Joe Nathan. Everything would have been different if she had given him sons.

Now she understood what Momma meant. They were a worry, all of them. Denise was the only one who was dependable. Had she made things worse yesterday, telling more lies? Could the police prove Denise had been here if she didn't tell them? What had she done?

CHAPTER
18

The elementary schools were letting out by the time Marti went to see Vera Holmes. Yellow buses pulled into the low-income apartment complex where Vera lived, and children swarmed out, laughing and shouting. Unlike the densely populated housing projects in Chicago, these were twelve-unit, three-story buildings with patches of winter brown grass outside and playground equipment that was still intact. The odor of urine and dirt greeted Marti as soon as she opened the front door. Some things stayed the same, she thought. Vera lived on the third floor. There were no elevators and the lighting was poor, but the doors had peepholes.

A short, slender woman wearing a Malcolm X T-shirt and jeans opened the door. There was no chain or dead bolt. "You're that police officer?"

"Detective MacAlister," Marti said, holding out her shield.

Vera turned off a small black-and-white TV. The apartment was nicer than Marti had expected. Sparsely furnished, but clean. White curtains framed a large window, and although there wasn't any sunshine, daylight made the room seem cheerful. A laundry basket was filled with children's toys, and dolls sat in chairs at a small table.

A textbook was open on the coffee table and beside it lay a pocket calculator.

"Are you in school?" Marti asked.

"Yes." Vera seemed reluctant to speak and twisted the bottom of her T-shirt.

"What are you studying?"

"Accounting."

"That sounds interesting. Where?"

"College of Lake County. I'll have my associate's in the spring."

Marti nodded toward the toys. "And you're doing this and raising a child?"

"My sister watches her for me."

"Good for you. It's not easy."

Vera smiled, but didn't look up.

"And you've been helping Deacon Hamilton with the bookkeeping at Mount Gethsemane?"

"Mostly I just run errands, pick up the books, make bank deposits, mail checks, things like that."

"How did you get the job?"

"Deacon Hamilton recommended me. He knew my mother years ago."

"So you knew Deacon Hamilton for a long time."

Vera rubbed the back of one hand with the palm of the other. "Yes."

Marti had checked the list of names from the guest book at the wake as well as the list Deacon Franklin had helped the uniform compile the night Hamilton's body was found. Vera had come to the house, but had not gone to the wake.

"How often did you see Deacon Hamilton?"

Vera worried the hem of the T-shirt again. "I took the books to him on Tuesday, after I'd recorded everyone's offering and deposited Sunday's collection. I picked them up Wednesday night. Last Wednesday there was a deacons' board meeting, so he brought the books to church."

"Did you see him Wednesday night?"

"Yes, he gave me the checks."

"How was he?"

She clasped her hands together. "I think he and Sister Hamilton had been arguing."

"What makes you say that?"

"The way they were looking at each other. They were angry. Sister Hamilton was wiping her face. She'd been crying. I was kind of embarrassed. I made like nothing was wrong."

Marti was certain that if asked, Gladys would deny this. Gladys wasn't too forthcoming with the truth.

A little girl came into the room. Vera hurried over and scooped her up, settling the child on her lap.

"Did you have a good nap, Tiffany?"

The child nodded, watching Marti with big, brown eyes. She was a pretty child, with her hair plaited in dozens of braids that hung below her shoulders.

For the first time since Marti arrived, Vera made eye contact. "Can you say hello to Detective MacAlister?" she said to the child.

Tiffany didn't say anything.

"It's okay, sweetie, Officer MacAlister isn't a stranger, she's a police officer. You can talk to her."

Tiffany put her thumb in her mouth.

"You're a very pretty little girl," Marti said. "How old are you?"

"She was four in August," Vera said.

A little younger than Zaar, Marti thought. But unlike Zaar, this child was loved.

"Do you want to go play?" Vera asked.

After a little coaxing, Tiffany occupied herself with the dolls, but every few minutes she stopped and looked at Marti.

"You have to be so careful," Vera said. "Teach them not to talk with anyone they don't know, not to go with anyone ever, not even a neighbor, stay right with you when you go somewhere. You can't be too careful anymore."

Watching Tiffany, Marti thought that perhaps Vera had been overzealous—but she did have a point, you couldn't be too careful anymore.

"Vera, did you know of any disagreements or arguments or just bad feelings between Deacon Hamilton and anyone else?"

"He wasn't friendly with anyone. Sometimes he and Deacon Gilmore or one of the other deacons didn't agree about something, like fixing something at the church or painting or remodeling the kitchen. Deacon Hamilton didn't like spending money. If the deacons' board didn't agree, though, it was decided by Deacon Franklin and the pastor. I don't know of anything else. Deacon Hamilton didn't hardly bother with nobody outside of church, at least not as far as I know."

"Where were you Friday night?" Marti asked.

"Me and Tiffany stayed with my sister," answered Vera. She seemed uneasy and looked away when she spoke.

On her way out, Marti checked the door. "I don't think this lock is providing enough security, Vera. Here's a number to call to have a dead bolt installed. It's a church. They don't charge. It's also a service for the elderly, but tell them I told you to call and they'll come over in a couple of days."

"Thanks." Vera smiled nervously as she accepted Marti's card. Tiffany smiled, too. They both seemed relieved to see Marti go.

Marti called the Reverend Douglas and went to meet with him in his office at the church. Degrees, certificates, and photographs filled the walls of the study—not just pictures of the family, but also of the reverend with the current and previous mayors, the city council, church officials Marti couldn't identify, Walter Mondale and Hubert Humphrey, and a player, now retired, from each of Chicago's major sports teams.

The Reverend Douglas came from behind the desk and led the way to two easy chairs by the window. Looking out, Marti could see the side of the church with the stained-glass window of Jesus in the Garden of Gethsemane, sweating blood.

The reverend spoke first. "How's your investigation coming along?"

"This Sunday you could remind your congregation that 'the truth shall set you free.' "

He gave her a quizzical stare, then smiled. "Maybe I'll do that."

"Were you at the deacons' board meeting Wednesday night?"

"I was available. They didn't ask me to join them."

"But you did see Henry?"

"He brought the books." He thought for a minute. "I got the impression he wasn't feeling well. He wasn't the most talkative person, but he hardly spoke at all on Wednesday. Someone else commented on that too. He didn't look well at all."

"Did anyone notice anything else?"

"Should they have?"

Marti shrugged. "Let me know if you hear anything. I just visited Vera Holmes."

He frowned. "She's not the reason for the sermon suggestion?"

"No, not at all."

"Good. We have a small committee here called Sarah's Circle. It's named for Vera's mother. Sarah Holmes died of cancer about nine years ago. She was sick most of her life, lived on welfare, really had to struggle to raise those two girls. In Sarah's Circle we try to recognize single parents like her who have such a hard time just surviving, and do something practical to help. Sometimes it's school supplies and clothes for the kids. Sometimes it's a trip to the beauty shop for mom or shoes or clothes so dad can dress for a job interview."

Marti thought of what Miss Hannah had said about Henry. "Did Henry Hamilton ever help Vera's mother?"

"No." The reverend seemed puzzled. "Not that I know of. Why would he?"

Yes, Marti agreed. Why would he.

CHAPTER
19

It was close to five o'clock when Marti arrived at the brick Tudor house the DeVeaux sisters shared. Camille DeVeaux was a schoolteacher and wasn't home yet. Her sister Eloise had taken early retirement and ran a small business at home baking cakes to order. Marti noticed the alarm system right away, glanced into the living room, and understood why—lots of antiques. The house smelled of vanilla and brown sugar. Two pecan pies were cooling on a counter. As Marti watched, Eloise spread white icing on the bottom layer of a wedding cake.

Eloise spoke with a musical Jamaican lilt. "Now, I've got to tell you, Officer, Denise and I are friends. I'm a bit older than she is, but we are close. So, you can ask me whatever you like. Whether or not I answer you is another matter entirely."

Marti smiled.

Eloise DeVeaux was at least fifty-five. Her hair was cut in an old-fashioned pageboy, her hips were broad and her bosom large. Her skin was smooth and brown. No wrinkles, just laugh lines. "Now, I called Denise after I spoke with you and she said to tell you whatever you wanted to know, but I will use my own discretion about that."

"That's fine." Marti liked her already.

"So, exactly what is it that you would like to know?"

"Whatever you'd like to tell me."

Eloise aligned a second layer of cake, picked up the spatula she was using to spread the icing, then stopped to look at Marti, one hand on her hip. "Denise says I should answer your questions, that you will find out who killed that man. But if I told you what I wanted to, I would say nothing." She scooped up some icing, began spreading it.

At the far end of the room a gleaming mahogany table was set with two lace placemats. Silver rings held linen napkins. Dozens of photographs were crowded on a matching sideboard. Christenings, school pictures, graduations, weddings, first communions. Students, Marti wondered, or relatives?

"How long have you known Denise and her family?"

"Since I am a teenager and they were children."

"You and Denise have always been close?"

"Yes. I baby-sat for Gladys before she got married."

"What about Belle and Terri?"

"Belle, that girl is too fast. And Terri, she is too much like her father. She appreciates nothing. Everything is her due. Denise I always thought would be a teacher. She tried social work, then she becomes a juvenile probation officer. It suits her, this job. She brings it home, but . . ." She shrugged. "I think it is the kind of job that you have to bring home, at least sometimes."

"She brings it here, to you?"

"Yes, to me and Camille."

"That's good."

Eloise paused to look at her again. "You like Denise?"

"Yes."

"That is good, too." All five layers were iced before she spoke again. "That marriage, it was not good for any of them. I do not know what happens in that house. But all of them, they change. Denise, she becomes very quiet, reads too much, plays too little. Belle, she becomes an exhibitionist. And Terri." She shook her head. "Terri. I think that girl must be crazy. But why are they this way? That I do not know. Denise, she never tells me. I am just glad that she survives and she works with children."

"Denise didn't like her stepfather," Marti said.

"No, she did not. And I am not sure that you will find anyone who did. That does not mean she killed him, any more than it means that all of the other people who did not like him killed him. You will not get too far, my friend the detective, if you operate on that theory."

"What happened between him and Gladys?"

Eloise began making rosettes. When twelve were lined up on wax paper, she put down the cone of icing and went to the sideboard. She pulled several photo albums from a drawer and flipped through them.

"Here," Eloise said, pointing to a smiling young woman with two little girls dressed alike in organdy pinafores.

"Denise and Belle," Marti said. They looked about two and four. "With Gladys?"

"With Gladys. Now, you tell me what that man did. Belittled her, I think. Or threw the other man or her past or something else into her face every day. You need to go see Gladys's mother. She's in a nursing home now. She cannot remember anything that has happened in the last thirty years and that includes what happened five minutes ago. Some days she recalls nothing at all and does not know her own children. Sometimes she remembers enough to curse Gladys for having illegitimate children, or to tell Belle and Denise that they are bastards. Go. See that woman. Then ask yourself how it was that Gladys could smile."

She picked up the cone of icing, made more rosettes. "Joe Nathan, it was," she said. "Joe Nathan Watkins is why she could smile. And Henry? Go see Gladys's mother. Nobody else does anymore, except Dolly."

Camille arrived a few minutes later. Her hips were broader than Eloise's, her smile wider, her Jamaican accent as musical, making Marti think of white sand and clear, blue water and warm sun. Camille went to the counter and poured coffee, bringing some to Marti.

"You offer our guest nothing, Eloise. You are upset perhaps because this involves Denise? You are going to use those two rosettes? They are not perfect." She scooped them up with one finger. "Ummm. But your icing. Always good."

"I do not think it is Gladys who did this," Camille said. "It would be good for everyone if it was Terri, but she is so fat now it's a wonder she can move at all, let alone go to her father's house and kill him. Stupid child, always pregnant, always sick. Crazy, that one. Eloise, it looks like you are anxious to finish that cake. Is it the one for Deborah's daughter?"

"Mmhmm."

"Then do take your time. She is so picky about

everything. One leaf a little crooked and she will want a refund and the cake as well." Camille turned to Marti. "Why is it that someone could not have sneaked into the house, killed the old man, and sneaked out? Must it be Gladys or Denise or Belle or Terri who did it? Why is it that it must always be someone in the family? Nobody liked that old man. I'm sure it could be somebody else."

"What were Belle and Denise like before Gladys got married?" Marti asked.

Camille considered her reply. "Denise was shy, quiet, but friendly and always ready to help. Belle was always outgoing, big smile, not a bit shy, and she had that beautiful voice, even as a child. By the time she was six, though, what a difference. She would sit on men's laps uninvited. She would pull up her dress and show you her undergarments. She was much too precocious for her age. And when she got older, she would do anything to shock you, like cutting the elastic in her slip so it would slide off while the choir was coming into the church. She was such a beautiful child, so much personality. It is such a shame, what she has become. 'The fruit doesn't fall far from the tree,' Gladys's mother would say, not realizing that she had to be talking about herself and Gladys as well."

Marti felt a headache beginning at her temples, and a vague feeling of depression. She had probably just been given a profile of an abused child.

She would stop by the nursing home and see Gladys's mother, complete her reports, and go home. She needed to be with her children.

Marti had passed the nursing home on Jefferson Street many times but had never been inside. The bright yellow walls offered a cheerier greeting than the harried aide at the nurses' station, who gave her a dour look and pointed in the general direction of Mrs. Stevens's room.

"What do you want? Who are you? Get out of my room!"

Mrs. Stevens wasn't friendly either, but she did seem coherent. Coppery skin, high cheekbones, and dark, deep-set eyes proclaimed her Indian ancestry. A single white braid hung down her back. Wisps of hair framed her face. She was so thin she looked emaciated.

"Did you bring me any food?" she whispered.

"No. Is there something you want?"

"Hopping John."

"I'll tell Gladys."

The woman gave her a blank look. "Gladys? No. Don't tell anyone who works here. They put drugs in the food so I'll sleep all the time. I can't eat anything they serve."

"Maybe Belle could bring you something."

"Whore!" she said.

"What about Denise?"

Again the woman didn't seem to recognize the name.

"Gladys is your daughter," Marti explained. "Belle and Denise are your granddaughters."

"Whore!" she said again.

"Who?"

"Gladys." Mrs. Stevens put her hand to her mouth and giggled, then whispered, "Gladys finally went and got herself married. But I told him anyway. I did. Trifling, that girl is. Willful from the day she was born. I told him just how to keep her in line."

"What did you tell him?"

The old woman giggled again. "That Joe Nathan didn't ever love her. That he would never leave that wife of his for her. That he didn't even want Gladys coming around. Joe Nathan didn't want no parts of none of them. And neither did I."

When Marti left, Gladys's mother was laughing and drooling from one side of her mouth. The sour-faced nurse asked what she had said to put Mrs. Stevens in such a good mood. Marti told her the truth, that she had no idea.

At eight o'clock Wednesday night, Marti was in her office staring out the window, watching a few stray snowflakes drift by, when the phone rang. It was Vera Holmes.

"I tried to reach you at home. Your daughter told me you were still at work. I hope I'm not bothering you."

"Of course not," Marti lied. She had to type the day's reports before she could leave. Vik was on his way out the door. She motioned him back. "Would you like me to come over, Vera?"

"I . . . no . . . please don't."

It was something Vera couldn't say in person.

"It's about . . . well, Deacon Hamilton. You see, when my mother was sick, Mrs. Hamilton came to see her. She even helped me feed her and bathe her and change her and make the bed. Mrs. Hamilton was so good to my mother and, well, she didn't know . . . and she was so kind to us."

As Marti listened, she became increasingly certain that Gladys did know whatever Vera was trying to tell her.

"Deacon Hamilton helped me get this job. He used to help my mother, too. He would come to our house, bring food. My mother was never well. We were on public aid all my life. We'd get surplus food. Deacon Hamilton would bring steak and pork chops and ice cream and orange juice, things we hardly ever got to eat."

Marti waited for her to continue.

"There was just me and my sister. My mother would have to go to the doctor, or to the public-aid office. He would baby-sit for her."

Marti felt the muscles in her stomach tighten. "How old were you?"

"Almost five. My sister was almost four. He would put her down for a nap. When she was asleep we would . . . play . . . games. I couldn't tell my mother. . . . When Sissy was five, she had to play too. It wasn't for long. He stopped coming after a couple of years. And he kept helping my mother, afterwards. He would send money or have food delivered. My mother thought he was a wonderful man."

"What kind of games did he play, Vera?"

Marti waited, but Vera didn't answer.

"Did he sexually abuse you?"

"Yes. I won't have to tell anyone else, will I?"

"I think you should talk to Reverend Douglas, or his wife. How old are you, Vera?"

"Thirty. Why?"

She gave the impression of being at least five years younger. "I was just wondering. May I discuss this with Reverend Douglas, if I have to?"

"I'd rather he didn't know."

"Vera, Deacon Hamilton might have 'helped' someone else who had little girls. I need to know."

For a moment Vera said nothing, then gave a deep sigh. "If you have to."

When Marti hung up, she felt like she would vomit if she so much as drank water. "Hamilton sexually abused her."

"Vera?" Vik said.

"And her sister. When they were about five years old. God, they were babies."

Vera's little girl was almost four and a half. And Henry had begun helping Vera. Had Vera thought Tiffany was next? Would she have killed Hamilton to protect her daughter?

C H A P T E R
20

Marti went to see Deacon Gilmore again on Thursday. She had tried all morning to locate Della Blake without success. Reverend Douglas thought Mrs. Blake had lived in one of Gilmore's apartments.

Gilmore was in the small, fenced-in yard behind his house. The grass was brown but it was the only place on the block where any grass grew. Gilmore was putting beer and soda cans and liquor bottles that had been tossed over the fence into a garbage bag.

"Basement window got broke," he said. "Kids playing with rocks."

Marti could see the fresh putty where he had put in a new pane of glass.

"Next thing you know they'll be going in through the broken window to find the rock," Gilmore said. "Along with anything else I might have lying around."

He pulled at the paper that was tangled in the fence. He was wearing an old army greatcoat that was at least one size too big. "How's it going? You getting close to finding out who did it?"

"Did Henry have any kind of a disagreement with anyone lately?"

"Not about anything in particular. He was sick enough to be cantankerous all of the time instead of some of the time, but we was used to that. Nobody took offense."

"Were you at last Wednesday night's meeting?"

"Of course."

"Did you see Gladys?"

He seemed about to say something, hesitated, and looked away. "No. But I think she was there."

Did he know of the argument Vera had mentioned? "How was Henry?"

"Ornery, same as always."

Marti turned so that her back was to the wind. "Did he get along with the other board members?"

"For the most part. Henry didn't make it easy to like him. The younger deacons had a lot of patience."

"And even though he didn't have any close friends, he didn't have any enemies either?"

"None that I know of."

"What did he do besides go to church?"

"Not much this past year or so, not much since he retired, as a matter of fact. He was serious about taking life easy. He'd go fishing, maybe, or take a walk. He liked to walk. He probably tinkered around the house, same as me."

"Did he have any fishing buddies?"

"Henry didn't have no buddies, fishing or not. He went alone."

"Did he have any women friends?"

Gilmore looked at her, squinting. "At seventy? Henry took a lot of pride in being an upright man before the Lord."

Marti heard the irony in his voice. "The way you say that makes me wonder."

"The older he got, the more upright he got, Henry did. He was good at looking down on those of us less righteous than he thought he was."

"You weren't the best of friends," Marti said.

"And we weren't enemies, either. We had a job to do, build that church and keep it sound and solvent. We did that for over thirty years. We didn't have to be best friends, we just had to take care of that church."

The wind gusted and Deacon Gilmore turned up his collar and moved closer to the house. "I do this every day. Got to pick up around front next."

"I'm trying to locate Della Blake. Reverend Douglas thought she used to be one of your tenants. Do you know where she lives now?"

He scratched his head. "Last address I had was over on Preston, but that was a good while ago. I think it was eight-ten, or maybe eight-twenty." The wind gusted again, and he ducked his head. "Got to get out of this. Catch a cold."

Marti watched as he walked to the stairs with the greatcoat flapping against his legs, then she headed back to her car.

Mrs. Blake had moved again, but a neighbor directed Marti three blocks south, to a house that had been converted into apartments.

"I don't know why you've come," Della Blake said as she led Marti into a small living room. She was about Gladys's age and walked with a cane. "I have nothing to say about Henry Hamilton or anyone else in that family."

The couch felt like someone had put a board under the cushions. One leg was missing and that end was supported by books. An afghan was tossed over the back and another was tossed over one arm of the sofa, as if Mrs. Blake had been lying down.

She took a chair by the window as Marti settled on the sofa. A basket of yarn was near her feet. "I try to never look back," she said.

"Mrs. Blake, I understand your position, but I

need to know what you know about Henry Hamilton."

"I don't want to get involved. I haven't even seen any of them in years."

"I respect that, but I need to know why you chose not to marry him, and if that decision was influenced by the fact that you had three young daughters."

The widow leaned forward, gripping the cane. "I have a right to privacy."

"There were other women who had daughters."

"And somebody killed him. I don't want to help you find out who that was. He deserved to die."

"Why?"

"Henry Hamilton, that man." She spoke so softly that Marti had to lean forward to hear her. "He fondled my oldest daughter."

She trembled. Marti thought it might be from anger.

"How old was she?" Marti asked.

"Six. She was six years old. I went to his commanding officer. They wouldn't tell me anything. The military protects its own. But he left the service right after that. I always thought there was something else. Something they didn't tell me. That he had done it before."

Intentional or not, Mrs. Blake had gotten revenge. "Did Henry ever do anything to retaliate? He was three years short of retirement."

"He caused me to lose my job, too. I'm not sure how. I was a housekeeper for a doctor who lived in Lake Forest. I was let go two weeks after he left the service, right about the time he married Gladys."

"Where is your daughter now?" Marti asked.

"She lives in Virginia. She married a sailor. She never comes here. I go to see her. We were never close, not after what happened."

The cane thumped softly as Mrs. Blake got up and walked to the window. "I tried, I tried to do something. I truly did. I went to Gladys . . . not then, not soon enough, not until Belle became such a problem, and Denise, that sweet little girl, became so quiet. I told Gladys what had happened. But Gladys, she told me how wonderful he was, what a good provider, what a kind and gentle man. I told her that didn't sound much like the man I knew. And she laughed, said that was why he married her and not me."

There was almost a pleading expression in her eyes as she looked at Marti. "I tried. I really did try. Gladys didn't believe me. I didn't know what else to do. I tried, Officer MacAlister. I did what I could. Gladys just wouldn't believe me."

Marti drove by Mount Gethsemane Church before returning to the precinct. The Reverend

Douglas was in his car, waiting to turn onto Austin Drive, when she pulled up alongside him.

"I need to talk with you."

They went to his study and sat in the two easy chairs by the window. As she looked out at the multicolored stained-glass Jesus, Marti told the reverend everything she had found out about Henry Hamilton.

Watching him react was like watching a storm slowly gathering overhead. His eyes grew dark, his body tensed as if he wanted to leap from the chair. She didn't have to tell him as much as she did, but he was a minister. He had to respect everyone's right to confidentiality, and he would. Marti needed to tell this to someone.

"Little Vera," he said. "And Sissy. And Allison Blake. Denise too, and Belle, but not Terri, surely not his own child."

"She's the reason I first suspected it."

"How could we be so close and not know?" He stared out the window until the furrows in his face became smooth and his hands stopped gripping the arms of the chair. "I will attend to this, Sister MacAlister. I don't know what I will be able to share with you, or require anyone else to share with you. But these women need healing, and I will seek them out."

Marti felt as if he had lifted a hundred-pound sack from her shoulders.

C H A P T E R

21

Marti got back to the precinct in time to talk with Slim and Cowboy. "I've got a sex offender who seeks out women with daughters who are about five to seven years old."

Cowboy considered that while he opened a pack of gum. "Pedophile."

"Yes. Give me a profile."

Slim ambled over to her desk. "You want a profile of a pedophile?" He gave her a languid smile. "You can't resist me any longer, can you, MacAlister? You're transferring to Vice."

"I'd rather work with a lunatic."

Slim winked. "I won't tell Vik you said that."

"Tell me about pedophiles."

"Are we discussing anyone I know?"

"Slim!"

"Okay, okay. Odds are, you know a pedophile. Statistically, there are more of them around than you realize. It can be a kind of low-profile activity. The arm around the shoulder and the hand that drops to the chest. The accidental touch of the legs or genitals. The voyeur who inadvertently goes into a room where a kid is likely to be undressed. Sometimes that behavior never accelerates into anything else. Then, there are the more overt actions."

He stopped smiling. "When it comes to sex offenses, the child is always exploited. Always. Last summer I went to some of my nephew's Little League games. I noticed that the pitcher seemed to be acting a little odd. So, I investigated. Come to find out, the kid is trying to please the coach. The guy liked to check his muscle development when the kid was showering or changing his clothes. Coach promised to help the kid get to the minors if he kept his mouth shut. This kid is thirteen. Is he old enough to understand what's going on? Yes. Is he exploited? Damned right. When I tell his old man, the guy is in shock, says the coach was going to help his kid go pro."

While Slim was talking, Cowboy stuffed several sticks of gum in his mouth and chewed until they were a manageable blob. "I hate pedophiles," he said. "They target a specific age group, and they do anything they can to gain access. They develop patterns of behavior. . . . Remember the guy who was a telephone lineman and had those mirrors so he could look in places like school bathroom windows? Sick. They establish occupations, plan careers, and make social choices so they can be around the kids they want. And they're very specific in their preferences."

"How many adults are there at Joanna's high school? A couple hundred?" Slim said. "Not just teachers or coaches. There are security guards, delivery people, kitchen workers, custodial staff. Ask her if there's one who's touchy-feely or who likes watching certain things that kids do. And it's not always a male."

"We're not talking about pats on the back or friendly hugs," Cowboy said. "Kids know when the touching is not appropriate. They get uncomfortable the same as we do."

They sat for a few minutes without speaking. Marti realized how often everyone joked about vice cops and decided not to tease Cowboy or Slim when they got their next indecent exposure case. Then she thought about what Slim had said about Joanna's school.

By six-thirty, Marti had finished writing her reports. She could go home early tonight. She smiled thinking about it. She had moved to Lincoln Prairie after Johnny died because Sharon, her best friend since kindergarten, lived here. Sharon was a teacher, recently divorced. When Marti moved in and began sharing expenses,

Sharon was able to quit her second job and be home after school to care for her own daughter and Marti's two kids. It was a great arrangement for them both.

By seven o'clock, Marti was settled on the couch with Theo on one side and Joanna on the other. Bigfoot, their dog, was asleep at her feet. Sharon and her daughter were in the recliner. They were having a Whoopi Goldberg film festival and had rented her favorites: *Jumping Jack Flash, Burglar,* and *Sister Act.* Mugs of mulled cider scented the room.

Marti looked at Theo, saw Johnny in the cleft of his chin and the perfect arch of his eyebrows.

"Here, Ma, have some." He reached for a bowl of popcorn, and Marti took a handful.

"You have any supper yet?" Joanna asked.

"I had a piece of that vegetarian pizza you made. It wasn't bad."

Joanna nudged Bigfoot out of the way and sat at her mother's feet. She gave Marti a brush and unbound her long auburn hair so Marti could brush out the tangles. Marti recalled sitting this way with Momma. After the movies ended, Marti carried a sleeping Theo to his bed, then went to Joanna's room.

"I'm going to clean up, Ma," Joanna promised as Marti stepped over socks, gym shoes, yesterday's jeans and T-shirt, and her basketball uniform.

Marti didn't say it, but thought to herself that Joanna could be so meticulous that if she didn't have at least one bad habit, she'd be impossible to live with. "I need to ask you something," Marti said. "Is there anyone at your school who's too familiar with the kids? Boys or girls?"

Joanna seemed embarrassed. "Ma, you've never asked a question like that before." She didn't say it didn't happen.

"Why don't you tell me about things like that? I'm a cop."

"Ma, it's kind of dumb. I'm smart enough to stay away from him."

Marti remembered Joanna talking about her drivers' ed course. "It's Mr. Knowles, isn't it? That's why you had me switch you to another instructor."

"Other parents know about him, Ma. Teachers too. They don't do anything."

"Joanna, tell me. I don't know what I can do. But I will do something. Some kids don't know how to stay away."

"I forget sometimes, about your being a cop. Not really, but you know. I don't think 'My mom's a cop, she can do this or that.' And I try not to ask you to blue-shirt people."

"Well, ask me. I don't mind throwing my weight around."

C H A P T E R
22

Denise pulled back the curtain and looked out at the trees that surrounded her house. Mist and fog shrouded everything. Looking out on nights like this, she always thought back to her first trip to South Carolina. Her great-grandmother's house was set way back in the woods. The taxi drove along a rutted dirt road, and the bare trees loomed tall and scary, with winter ground-fog swirling about gnarled trunks and Spanish moss hanging from the branches like thick, ropy spiderwebs.

That tiny old house, with an outhouse and a water pump outside, became a haven those two weeks she was there. And that dear woman, who smelled of camphor and almost always smiled and who looked so much like Momma, became everything that Momma was not.

In her great-grandmother's house, she wasn't

too old to be held by those thin, loving arms. She wasn't too big to sit on that apron-covered lap. She drank chamomile or sassafras tea and ate eggs she took from the hens, and yams baked in the coals of the wood-burning stove. She had never eaten yams that tasted as good since. When it was time to leave she had clung to that old woman, crying and begging to stay.

Her great-grandmother had not understood why she wasn't eager to get back to her new daddy and her new home, and Denise couldn't tell her. Belle was clamoring for the bus ride back to Illinois. He hadn't started sending for Belle yet. Just her.

Her great-grandmother had died in that house that winter. Even now she wished she had been there to ease that old woman's passing, or just keep her from being alone. When Henry died, she could not find enough forgiveness to wish the same for him, but she should not have left him.

Sometimes, she thought she could remember the time before Henry, thought she remembered gold flashing when her real daddy smiled, thought he laughed deep and often, and his breath smelled of peppermint. It was probably just her imagination. She knew who he was, Joe Nathan Watkins. Sometimes she drove past his barbershop, but not deliberately. She had never sought him out and didn't think she would know him if she saw him. She had grown past the time when she needed a father, and besides, he had never wanted her or Belle. Instead there was Henry Hamilton.

Denise closed the curtain. Henry had taken more from her than innocence or virginity. He had robbed her of herself, until she couldn't look in a mirror, until she hid her body in a layer of fat so that other men would not look at her or desire her. She still denied herself the gifts of husband and children. And although she understood all of this, she could not change it. She had bought this land, built this house, and had that cracked and aged photograph of her great-grandmother restored so that at least, at night, she could come home.

The room was dark except for the light from flames that burned low in the fireplace. She went to the hearth, held out her hands to the warmth. She still could not separate what she had allowed her life to become from what he had caused. Not even therapy could bring her farther than she was. He had only abused her for two years. Was her therapist right? In spite of all the abused children she had worked with over the years, did she still blame herself? What was going to happen to her now that she had so much more to blame herself for?

CHAPTER
23

On Friday morning, Marti called Denise to make sure she was in her office, then walked the short half block from the precinct to the county building. The wind was raw and cold off Lake Michigan, and before she turned the corner sleet was stinging her face. She couldn't remember the sun shining one day this month. Thanksgiving was just two weeks away. By then they would probably have snow.

Denise met her at the door. It was one of the two times that Marti could recall seeing Denise without a hat on. The other had been last Saturday night. Instead of the hat, a clunky necklace with carved and painted beads and animals drew Marti's attention away from Denise's body and back to her face.

Denise's office was actually a suite. A multi-purpose reception area had a corral filled with toys for very young children. Another room looked like it was used for play therapy, and another was a small classroom. The room Denise took her to was the most formal, with a desk and bookcase, two comfortable chairs, and a sofa.

"Nice place," Marti said.

Denise seemed uneasy as she circled the desk and sat down, clasping her hands in her lap. "When they set up that separate facility for child-abuse victims, we were included in the grant because so many abused kids are in the juvenile system. As you can see, we do some of everything here. Intake and interviews as well as baby-sitting siblings while we talk with parents and even tutoring three afternoons a week. We have classes for latchkey kids and self-defense and Alatot/Alateen/AA groups that each meet twice a week."

"Impressive," Marti said. "I had no idea your operation was this intense. Vik and I just know that you're the person to call when we get a juvenile. Neither one of us is very good with kids."

"But you are," Denise said. "You don't talk down to them." She went to a small refrigerator in the corner and took out a quart of orange juice. "The receptionist is in caffeine withdrawal. Some kind of health problem. The rest of us are trying to stay away from coffee until noon."

She didn't ask why Marti was there.

"What do you do about a high school teacher who's too familiar with the students?"

"How familiar?"

"Juvenile-type touchy-feely stuff. A hand accidentally caressing a breast. A squeeze of the thigh."

"It's called sexual harassment. There are professional women working in major corporations who can't deal with it effectively. Most kids just try to avoid teachers like that."

"That's what Joanna said. But it shouldn't be that way."

"Many things 'shouldn't be that way.' It's difficult to change them. You have to acknowledge them first."

"What do I tell Joanna? I've already told her I'd take care of it."

Denise smiled. "Oh, we can do something. I already know who you're talking about: Mr. Knowles. We don't have enough to bring charges. What he's doing is considered pretty inconsequential by too many adults. They're in the process of changing his schedule. He won't be teaching drivers' ed much longer."

"Do you think he's a pedophile?" Marti asked.

Glass rapped against wood as Denise put down her glass of juice.

"No. His behavior's too nonspecific. He's just your ordinary, garden-variety pervert. His type of behavior doesn't accelerate. It gives him a sense of power, a feeling of control. It puts him in the driver's seat in more ways than one. The girls are essentially helpless. He likes that."

"You say that so casually."

"There's worse," Denise said. "There's much worse."

"Like molesting five- and six-year-old girls?" Marti asked.

Denise walked to the window, looked out. "We get a lot of that."

"How do you help them?"

"It's difficult. We used to concentrate on building self-esteem. Now we try to empower the child, give them some control over their lives, give them choices, help them make good decisions, explain when it's appropriate to say no to an adult."

"What happens to the child who nobody knows about? This is a quiet, secret crime. I'll bet many children don't tell."

Denise didn't answer right away. "They die a little, I think." Her voice sounded wistful. "So much of who they could be is lost by the time they come here. You want to retrieve it somehow. But even at five or six, so much of their potential is lost."

Marti spoke very quietly. "Are you talking about someone you know?"

Denise turned. "Perhaps," she said, with that wry, rueful smile.

Even that admission was much more than Marti had expected.

After her meeting with Denise, Marti and Vik met with Janet Petrosky in her office at the coroner's facility. "How about some coffee?" Janet said. "I pulled everything on the Hamilton case yesterday afternoon and went over it before I went home."

Janet was a tall, middle-aged woman. Her blond hair, cut in precise layers, and her makeup, applied sparingly in the softest shades, gave an elegance to her plain, oval face. She served the coffee in mugs thick enough to be dropped on the floor without breaking. Marti thought they might have first seen use in some kind of an institution.

The office was sparsely furnished: two file cabinets, a desk with a stack of manila folders, a pencil holder, and a color photo of Janet standing beside a chestnut mare. The chairs for visitors had minimal padding and were uncomfortable enough to have come from the same place as the cups. On one wall was a large picture frame with cutouts for eighteen photographs. When Janet was elected coroner ten years ago, there had been fifteen unsolved murders countywide. Morgue shots of each victim were put in the frame and kept there until the case was solved. Whenever another homicide stayed open for a year, the victim's picture was added. Today, there were eight death-stilled faces in the frame, a silent reminder of effort that hadn't paid off yet.

"Congratulations," Marti said. "Is this your first grandchild?"

"Third, but the other two are boys. If Hamilton wasn't Denise Stevens's stepfather, I would have stayed in Oregon a few days longer."

"We're glad you're back." Marti held her mug with both hands. The coffee was strong and hot. "Can you give us any more information about the condition of Hamilton's digestive tract?"

"Rick Fields said you were concerned about that. He and Dr. Nichols are both very conservative in their approach to forensic medicine, but very thorough and competent."

"Hell of a lot of good that did us," Vik said. "They wouldn't tell us a damned thing other than the cause of death."

"Which is asphyxiation by suffocation," Janet said. "There were no secondary causes. That was it." She smiled. "You two just want to know every single detail. And that means waiting for lab results."

Janet opened a manila folder. "His medical records are right here." She gave them each a copy. "And they do get your attention. Hamilton was brought to the emergency room half a dozen times within the past year and a half and diagnosed as having gastroenteritis—-that's often a nonspecific diagnosis until they pinpoint the cause. He never followed up with a visit to the doctor, although recently he did make several appointments that were never kept. He had ample health insurance, so that wouldn't have been a consideration."

Janet tapped the folder. "He should have been a robust, healthy, seventy-year-old man. There was no heart or lung disease. He had minimal hardening of the arteries and minor degenerative disease in his joints, but there was nothing that would have killed him in the next twenty years. Those tumors were in fatty tissue, and cancer looks like what it is, angry, aggressive. The way these tumors are described, I'm almost certain they were benign."

Marti scanned the photocopied hospital reports. The family seemed to assume that Hamilton was a very sick man, and he certainly looked to be in poor health. But except for these trips to the hospital, he had no contact with a physician, no specific diagnosis, no other medical intervention. Why had everyone, including Hamilton, done nothing?

"Puzzling, isn't it?" Marti said. "A lot of people don't like doctors, but most of them end up going to them anyway."

Vik shifted. "The taxpayers need to ante up for some new office furniture in here," he complained as he slapped his copies of the reports down on the desk. "How important is any of this?"

"That's for you to decide," Janet said. "You inquired about the possibility of poison, and based on this, that's a logical question. We won't know the answer until we get the test results back, and I don't know how important this is to your investigation. This has nothing to do with the cause of death, but it is possible that Hamilton ingested something poisonous."

"It could have been accidental," Vik said.

"Yes," Janet agreed. "We have had instances where someone ate something seemingly innocuous that wasn't."

"Could this have happened over an extended period of time, Janet?" Marti asked.

"I would say so."

"Then you'd think he'd catch on," Vik said. "Eat something. Get sick. Get smart."

"Not necessarily," Janet said. "It could be something that was used in cooking a variety of foods, for example."

Marti thought for a minute. "He's the only one who got sick."

"He died of asphyxiation," Vik said.

"I know," Marti said. "But this is puzzling. We can't ignore it."

"And we can't make a hell of a lot of sense of it, either," Vik complained. "Why couldn't he just have a heart attack? A lot of people do. Maybe if we figure out who sent the church choir over to destroy the evidence we'll have the perp. Sixty-five people passed through that room that night. It'll take six months just to sort through the fibers that were transferred."

"I wish we had the lab reports so we could resolve this."

"There's nothing to resolve, MacAlister. That isn't what killed him," Vik said. "We're having enough trouble trying to determine who held the damned pillow over his face."

Marti felt frustrated too. "We can't just ignore this," she said, waving the hospital records.

"Yes we can. We don't even have a solid motive," Vik reminded her. "Let's keep working on that."

"Stop squabbling," Janet chided, smiling. "I don't know if this will be a help or a hindrance, but if you think poisoning is a factor, I would err on the side of assuming we'll get positive results."

Marti and Vik had a two o'clock meeting with their boss, Lieutenant Dirkowitz. He would be out of town at a seminar the following week. "Dirty Dirk" earned his nickname while playing football for the Southern Illinois University Saluki about ten years ago. He was built like a linebacker—all muscle, no fat—and worked at maintaining his weight. He was drinking a diet pop when they went into his office.

Dirkowitz's only question about the Hamilton case was, "Does it look like it could be Denise Stevens?" They had to admit they didn't know. "Be discreet," he warned, which meant he wouldn't be pleased if Denise's name was bandied about as a suspect.

C H A P T E R

24

It was getting dark when Marti pulled up in front of the hair salon and barbershop that Joe Nathan Watkins owned. He lived upstairs in a spacious apartment with lots of windows. Containers from nearby take-out restaurants littered the kitchen. The wastebasket was full, and a garbage bag slumped beside it. Judging by the way the dishes were stacked, Marti guessed that Watkins was getting ready to load the dishwasher.

Gladys Hamilton seemed to have a preference for tall, slender men. Watkins was dark with short, kinky hair that was graying at the temples. She could see the resemblance to Denise and Belle, especially in his eyes, which were almond-shaped, large, and dark. Marti wondered about his relationship with his daughters, and what had happened between him and Gladys over the years.

Watkins moved a stack of newspapers from a chair to the floor so Marti could sit down, then sat across from her at the kitchen table. She could look straight through the house, past the dining room to the picture window in the living room that faced a busy four-lane street.

"Detective MacAlister." A gold tooth flashed as he spoke with a slow drawl. "You come to see me because old Henry Hamilton died."

Looking at him, Marti remembered Momma telling her that there wasn't nothing prettier than a pretty black man. Joe Nathan must have been pretty in his youth. He was still a good-looking man. "How well do you know Gladys Hamilton?"

He cocked his head to one side, raising his eyebrows, and shrugged. "I think you know that."

"Have you seen her lately?"

"No. Not since a couple of months after my wife died."

"When was that?" Marti asked.

He looked away. "Lallie passed a year and a half ago. May twenty-sixth. Brain aneurysm." He rubbed one knuckle with his thumb, stopped when he looked down at his hands. "I was sitting right here, watching her water her plants, she had lots of 'em. We was talking about going to Cancún. We was sort of joking about it being a place where young folks would go, and she was laughing. Then she stopped."

His voice was flat as he tried to distance himself from his grief. Marti could remember doing that for a long time after her husband died.

"We got married right out of high school," he said. "We lived here together for thirty-four years."

While she waited for him to speak again, Marti looked at a collection of plates on the wall in the dining room. She could make out the Statue of Liberty on one, palm trees on another. She didn't see any photographs. She wondered if they had children.

When Watkins didn't say anything else, Marti said, "How well did you know Henry Hamilton?"

"I didn't know him at all. I've seen him once or twice. Not in a long while. Man's dead. Newspaper said he died of undetermined causes. That must mean someone killed him, since you're here asking questions."

Marti didn't answer.

"Gladys called me Sunday afternoon and again this morning to see if you'd been here. Told me not to be telling nobody none of her business. I told her I don't owe her that, but I'd think on it." He folded back his sleeve and held up his arm to show Marti a long, curving scar. "Gladys did this right after I bought this place. We had to start over, me and Lallie. I told Gladys I couldn't see her no more. She told me I couldn't see them little girls again neither, that she was gonna get them a real daddy, and she did. Married Hamilton a couple of months later."

His thumb began worrying his knuckle again. "Back then, when I was seeing Gladys, there was a lot that a black man did that a black woman just put up with. Gladys would get in her sister's car with them little girls and drive by where we was living and toot the horn. Lallie, she made like they don't exist. It was years before I understood how much that hurt her. She couldn't have children of her own." He pointed to the scar. "I don't know how he died, but if Gladys did it, he knew what was about to happen."

"When's the last time you saw Gladys?"

"Like I said, she came here after Lallie died." He got up, walked about the room, paused by the window. "I hadn't seen her in years. Hard to believe how much she'd changed."

"What was she like when she was young?"

"Wild. Looking at her, you'd think she was that proper little lady her momma raised her to be . . . but she wasn't. And she was so little and so pretty. I really did believe she was just defying her momma, seeing me. I really did believe that's all it was."

When Gladys was a teenager, a pretty, light-skinned African American woman of moderate means with Gladys's social background didn't get involved with a poor, dark-skinned black man. It would have been the height of rebellion. And even though Joe Nathan would have been the envy of his friends, his family would not have been pleased, either.

"How did you meet her?"

Watkins returned to the table, looked at her for a moment, then sat down. "There was this bar over on Eureka, the Kit Kat Club. They never asked her for any identification. We was both young. I never did believe Gladys had any deep feelings for me. Maybe things would have been different if I had. I don't know."

He looked down at the table as he spoke. "Gladys came here after Lallie died and said that for all these years she'd loved me. She said she wanted us to be together again. I told her the truth. I never did have those kinds of feelings for her. If I didn't tell her that, she would have kept coming back. She got mad, real mad." He smiled. "I thought she was gonna stamp her foot like she did years ago, or slap my face, maybe even try to cut me again. But all that fire is gone." He shook his head. "Don't know what it was like for her, being married to that man, but he done taken all what she was when I knew her. She was right after all, defying her momma. Should have kept right on going against her. Henry be all that her family wanted for her. Respectable. But now there ain't nothing left of her at all that I might have even thought I coulda cared for."

After Marti left the apartment, she sat in her car for a few minutes watching as Joe Nathan turned the OPEN sign in the downstairs front window to CLOSED. Deacon Gilmore had said that Gladys was like Belle on the inside. Watkins had said pretty much the same thing. What had Gladys dreamed about all of these years if she did still love, or believe that she loved, Joe Nathan? Because Joe Nathan had destroyed that dream when he saw her the summer before. And according to Henry's medical records, that was when his health problems had begun.

C H A P T E R

25

Gladys sat in the living room, sipping wine. She had been trying to figure out her expenses, how much money she would need and how much she would have coming in. Henry had always taken care of that and she couldn't find the book he kept his records in. She hadn't opened an electric bill or gas bill as long as she lived here, and when the telephone bill came today she didn't even understand the charges. She wasn't sure, but it didn't seem like there was going to be enough for her to get along. Denise was going to go over everything for her and then explain it. Denise would help her if there wasn't enough money coming in, but she wanted to be able to look after herself.

Henry had figured out to the last penny how much money she would have. She was sure there wouldn't be enough left over to buy hats. Maybe it would have been better if he hadn't died so soon, but she had been happier the week before he died than she had been since she married him. He had been so tired, so weak. She had taunted him about being a helpless old man for an hour before he went out to the yard to prove that he wasn't. That had tired him out so much that he'd hardly touched his supper. He had given her such a look when he got up from the table, not of disgust or annoyance as he had so often in the past, but a look almost of . . . fear. She could still see his face.

Then he had accused her of flirting with Deacon Gilmore Wednesday night, as if she would ever be interested in him. Tired of being called a slut, she had followed him down the hall and into his room, telling him about Joe Nathan. When she ran out of all the stories that were true, her times with Joe Nathan before the girls were born and before she married Henry, she had told him all the stories she wished had been true, all the things she had thought about and wished for over the years—seeing Joe Nathan when she was supposed to be out shopping, being with Joe Nathan when Henry thought she was at church, leaving church early on Tuesday nights to spend a few minutes with Joe Nathan. Seeing him now that his wife was dead. Seeing him whenever she pleased.

She put her glass on the table without worrying about leaving a ring. She smiled. Henry had never allowed spirits in the house. She used to drink with Joe Nathan. She would sneak out of the house and hurry down to Greatflower Street and hop on the streetcar and meet him at that little speakeasy on Eureka. Because she was with him, nobody ever asked her age. The Kit Kat Club—jukebox, dance floor, cigarette smoke, liquor, yelling to make yourself heard, a hundred people crowded into a space intended for half as many. How she loved that place. None of Momma's seditty friends would be caught dead there, which was fine with her.

Later, laughing and feeling fine, they'd leave the crowd and the noise and the music and the wine, and go to Joe Nathan's car, or maybe get real bold and go to Truman Park and find some soft grass to lie in halfway down the ravine. Or there was the beach, with boats dipping way out on the lake and lights flashing from the buoys and sand getting in her hair.

Joe Nathan. She had never gotten enough of him, never would. "The darker the berry, the sweeter the juice," folks used to say. Joe Nathan was sweet as they come. She would have to make Joe Nathan change his mind, now that Henry was dead. She had gone to him too soon after that wife of his had died. Guilt was a hard thing to live with. He still had too much guilt when she went there. She didn't have any guilt at all, not about Henry. She wished she had thought of more things to do to Henry, ways to make him sicker, sooner. She wished she had killed him sooner. Even if it meant not having enough money.

She picked up the glass. Empty, but the bottle was not. Maybe tonight she would put all the lights out. Maybe tonight she would sleep well. Old Henry was down in the ground now. Old Henry was gone. Gladys got up, poured more wine, drained the glass. She had danced half the night, her and Joe Nathan, then they had loved almost until morning. They would do that again. They would. He did want her no matter what he said. Even Deacon Gilmore had commented on her being a widow now and perhaps needing a little help around the house. Joe Nathan was a handyman, too. She giggled. Joe Nathan was handy with more than a workman's tools. There were so many things he could do with his hands.

She had called him again this morning and asked him not to talk to the police. He didn't say much, but she could tell he was worried about her. She would see him again soon, maybe next week.

Gladys stumbled a little as she walked through the house. She put out the light in the kitchen, but when she tried to leave the room, she could not leave it dark and turned the light back on. She went to the living room and poured just one more glass of wine, just so she could sleep. Then she sat in the chair in the corner, where she could see every part of the room, and put her feet up on the hassock. It wasn't as comfortable as her bed, but it would do.

CHAPTER

26

When Marti woke up Saturday morning, she went down to the kitchen and began making waffles. She seldom cooked these days, but there was something soothing and reassuring about measuring and pouring and mixing. It made her think of Momma and their times together in the kitchen. The first waffle had to be thrown out, but she could make them better than anyone else in the house. The second was better.

It wasn't long before Sharon came downstairs. The blue-and-turquoise paisley print of her voluminous caftan swirled as she clattered into the room wearing mules. She had replaced her bushy hairstyle with a weave in August. Dozens of braids looped behind her ears and cascaded down her back.

"Waffles. Lord, what time is it?" She checked her wrist, then squinted at the clock on the stove. "It's five-thirty-eight. And you're dressed and ready to go. Great. You've got plenty of time to make three waffles just for me."

"Take these." Marti mixed more batter. She did this at least twice a year and they would eat as many as she would cook.

"What's got you in such a good mood?" Sharon asked. "Did you figure out who killed Deacon Hamilton?"

"No, but I do have enough new information to broaden the investigation." Or narrow it down to Denise.

"It couldn't be Denise."

Marti didn't answer. She never went into much detail about a case with her friends, even when the identity of the primary suspects became this easy to figure out.

"A lot of people are praying over this," Sharon said.

"Don't stop now," Marti advised. Then she asked, "Why would anyone think it was Denise?"

Sharon hesitated. "Something happened that Friday before he died. I don't know what, but . . . this is really just gossip, Marti."

"Tell me anyway."

"Somebody who works with her said Denise got a phone call just before she went home and she was furious."

"They don't know why?"

"It had something to do with hats."

Hats. Gladys had said something about hats in Gullah Saturday night. Gladys had bought a new hat on Saturday, while Henry lay dead in his bed. And Denise probably had a lot of hats, she wore them so often. "Does that mean anything to you?"

Sharon reached for the maple syrup. "I started something, didn't I. The important thing is what it means to you. Can you tell me?"

Marti shook her head.

"Well, I sure don't want to say anything else. But I guess I have to. I'm not sure why Denise wears hats all the time, it's only a must for church, but she always looks so pretty in them. Now Gladys, folks say she'd rather shop for a hat than eat. I don't know how that could be important."

"Maybe it isn't. I don't know."

"Lord, Marti, I'm sure glad it's you and Vik on this case. At least no matter how it turns out, I'll know that whoever you arrest is really the one."

Marti smiled at her. "Thanks."

Sharon put the syrup on the table. "Since you haven't made any coffee yet, let me."

"Don't knock my coffee, Sharon. I think it tastes great."

Sharon took care of the coffee and got out real butter. Joanna had insisted that they buy a buttery-tasting spread that didn't approach the real thing.

"Sharon, where do you keep that hid?"

"See the box of instant potatoes that nobody likes and nobody touches? I emptied it and keep the butter in there. But don't tell. And speaking of butter and other real food, Thanksgiving's a week from Thursday, last Thursday of the month, same as last year. I sure hope you've marked your calendar at work and you're planning to spend as much of the day as possible here at home. We are having one of our three annual soul food celebrations. No tofu, no bean sprouts. We will allow mashed rutabaga, but no broccoli, spinach or zucchini. And the only salads we'll be fixing are Waldorf and ambrosia. And Ben and Mike will be coming."

Marti poured another waffle. "Good."

"Good? Does that mean . . . ?"

"That means Ben and I are . . . becoming friends."

"Oh." Sharon sounded disappointed.

Marti thought back to the kiss she and Ben had exchanged the last time she saw him. "Good friends," she admitted. "Maybe."

She had not been avoiding him since. She had been busy.

"How good?"

"I'm not sure," Marti admitted. "I don't know how friendly I want to get."

"Then take it slow," Sharon said, surprising her.

"I thought you'd be urging me to hop into bed with him."

"No, that's what I do best. You and Ben are the cerebral types. I'm sure it'll be as much of an intellectual decision as an emotional one. That cuts down on the fun, but maybe the disappointments also."

Joanna stumbled into the kitchen at 6:25, still in pajamas. She was not a morning person and made a cup of herbal tea before speaking. "Waffles? What are you depressed about?"

"I just felt like cooking."

"You always want gooey sweet things when you're depressed, Ma."

"Kids aren't supposed to notice things like that."

"Be nice if you could come to my game tonight."

"Can't. I'm going to Chicago. Maybe next time."

Theo bounded into the room, dressed and ready for cartoons. "Wow, Ma, waffles! You made an arrest!"

"Not yet."

Bigfoot padded in behind Theo and nudged Marti's hand with his nose. "I suppose you want a waffle too?" She rubbed the spot between his eyes, then washed her hands and made more batter. "Theo, you take these. The next two are mine." Sharon's daughter always slept in on Saturday. "By the time Lisa wakes up I'll be long gone, but I'll make a couple that she can warm up." As she watched Joanna and Theo spreading butter and pouring syrup, she began humming.

When she got to the precinct Vik was already there. Forms were stacked on his desk in neat piles. He was snapping pencils in half.

"I thought you'd be glad that the Hamilton case is finally opening up," she said, wondering why he was upset.

"We're not going to have the lab results back for at least another week."

"But the cause of death was . . ."

"Asphyxia. I know." He snapped another pencil. "I can't stand not having all of the pieces."

The child molestation was bothering him.

"This might start getting pretty nasty, Vik. I came real close to getting an admission of molestation from Denise. I'm going to watch Belle sing tonight. And I intend to say something about it to her."

"I think we have stronger suspects, Danzel Whittaker, for one, if I could just come up with a motive. Don't write Vera Holmes off either, Marti. She had a child to protect."

So did Terri, if she realized it.

"I think something happened between Gladys and Henry at church Wednesday night. And I keep hearing something about hats. I doubt that

Henry was any friendlier at home than he was anywhere else. They didn't even sleep in the same room. It might not have taken much for Gladys to go back there and smother him." She remembered what Joe Nathan said about Gladys making sure Henry knew what was coming. "And I bet she would have woke him up."

"We need to know why." Vik snapped another pencil. His supply exhausted, he went to get more, trailing Slim and Cowboy when he came back.

"You're going to have to stop showering in that cologne, Slim, it's clogging my sinuses."

"Uh-oh," Slim said, backing away. "Must be that time of the month."

Cowboy checked his calendar. "Uh-uh. Not 'til sometime next week."

Marti chose not to respond.

"That sounds like sexual harassment," Vik said. He sounded genuinely angry. Marti was shocked.

"Oh, so you're unhappy this morning too, Jessenovik," Cowboy drawled. "Know what, partner?" he said to Slim. "I think we'd better get our butts out of here. Let's not even tell them what happened last night."

"The sweep on prostitutes?" Vik asked.

Slim grinned. "It was great. Seventeen arrests."

Marti wished working Homicide was that easy.

"Great. That should keep you in court most of next week."

"I take it progress is slow on the Hamilton case," Slim said.

"I suppose you know them, too," Marti said. Everybody around here knew everybody else, except her. Sometimes not having grown up in this town made her feel like an absolute outsider.

"I don't know Denise more than to say hello," Slim admitted. "But everyone knows Belle. That girl came right out of her slip one Easter Sunday. . . ."

"Palm Sunday," Marti corrected. "While the choir was marching to the front of the church."

Slim chuckled. "You heard that one already. Everybody remembers it, probably because we all knew Belle did it on purpose and nobody could figure out exactly how. Of course Belle has done worse. She was out in the school yard once, doing cartwheels without any underpants on. She did it real clever, too. Sometimes you got a glimpse, sometimes you saw nothing. She had to spend a lot of time practicing weird stuff like that."

"You ever date her?" Marti asked. "Are you close to the same age?"

"I'm younger. Not that it would have mattered. Belle was kind of loose. I left her alone. Didn't want to catch anything."

"She ever have anything to catch?"

"There were rumors."

"She doesn't seem like such a bad person," Marti said.

Vik looked up from the reports he was reading. "That's because you have a soft spot for drunks."

"Actually, she isn't," Slim agreed, ignoring Vik. "I've never known her to do anything to hurt anyone but herself. She's real good at self-destructing. She's a lounge singer, works at that dump in the city on Saturday night. And that girl can sing. The liquor hasn't done too much to her vocal cords yet. The rest of her is probably getting pickled in it, though." He shook his head. "Belle really isn't a bad person. She'll give you the shirt off her back, if she's wearing a shirt, or anything. She still strips sometimes, occasionally during her show. And she's still got a great set of boobs and a fantastic . . . um . . . a few other things ain't sagging too much yet, either."

"Female officer present," Vik reminded him.

"Mac's just a cop."

"Mac doesn't like being talked about in third person," Marti said.

C H A P T E R
27

Marti supposed the Starlight Lounge could be described as intimate instead of a hole-in-the-wall and picturesque rather than shabby, but it would require long leaps of imagination. At some point, maybe within the last ten years, the walls had been painted a deep red. Now the paint was peeling in places where dampness had seeped from the roof. Most of the upholstery in the booths was red also, and patched with plastic tape close to the same color. Mismatched chairs and tables were scattered across the linoleum floor. The room was long and narrow. The bar was near the entrance. At the opposite end of the room wooden pallets pushed together served as a stage. A grand piano and some sound equipment took up most of the space. Someone had recently mopped, and a sour odor tinged with pine still lingered.

Marti sat in one of the booths, facing the bar. She didn't like sitting with her back to the door, and she didn't want the exposure of sitting at a table. Ben sat across from her. When the bartender came over, she asked for a cola with a lime twist. Ben ordered a beer. The bartender, bald and potbellied, looked at her. "Problem, Officer?" he said, making her as a cop without seeing any ID.

"I've come to see Belle Stevens sing. Will she be here tonight?"

"Belle should be here any time now. She goes on at eight."

Marti squeezed the lime slice, stirred her drink with the swizzle stick, and tasted it.

"Think she'll show?" Ben asked.

"We'll give her until eight-thirty."

"Fair enough."

They hadn't said much on the drive down, but that wasn't unusual. Ben drove, and once or twice she had caught him looking at her with a bemused expression. She supposed they had crossed some line, or at least stretched the word *friendship* a bit, with that kiss the other night, but she wasn't sure. She still felt comfortable with him, and she wouldn't object if he kissed her again. What she didn't know was how far she wanted things to go. There had never been anyone else, just Johnny. He had been her childhood sweetheart, the only man she had kissed until now.

She had told him to remarry if anything happened to her. He had told her the same thing. Except for that, they hadn't discussed the possibility of dying. She thought of Browning's verse, "Grow old along with me! The best is yet to be. . . ." They had had the best, or so she thought. It just hadn't lasted long enough.

"What are you thinking about?" Ben asked.

"A friend of Sharon's came by with some jalapeño peppers this afternoon." That wasn't what she had intended to say. The peppers, pungent, with leaves still clinging, had brought back a sudden sharp memory of Johnny. For half a second she had almost expected him to walk into the room.

She had learned a lot about being alone. She had promised herself that she would wait until she was comfortable with loneliness before she decided how and if she would try to change things. She didn't feel comfortable with the circumstances surrounding Johnny's death. She couldn't believe it was suicide, but she couldn't prove it wasn't. That lack of resolution, after two and a half years, kept her in some kind of limbo. Emotionally, she thought she was adjusting, but the cop in her couldn't let go.

She tried to convince herself that loneliness was okay, but on those nights when she hadn't worked late and wasn't exhausted enough to fall asleep as soon as her head hit the pillow, she could almost touch the places that had been filled by Johnny's presence and were empty hollows in her life now that he was gone.

The door opened. Marti heard Belle's laughter before she saw her. A man came in first, tall and light skinned, carrying a saxophone case. He was the same man who had been in the bar when she'd talked with Belle last Sunday night. He was Belle's alibi. Seeing him with Belle tonight lent credence to that. He hadn't gone to the wake or the funeral. Marti tried not to compare him to a young Henry Hamilton, but the similarities were there. He looked young enough to be carded. He was followed by a short, brown-skinned woman with her hair dyed blond who was lugging in a larger instrument case. Belle entered last. She looked around, saw Marti, and waved. She had a drink in her hand when she came to the table. Ben excused himself and went outside.

"The boyfriend?" Belle asked, gesturing in Ben's direction. She had been drinking.

Marti shrugged.

Belle slipped off her fake fur coat. She was wearing a green dress that looked like it would burst at the seams if she sneezed.

"You see the guy I came in with?"

Marti nodded.

"He's my alibi."

"You told me."

Belle looked at as if she didn't remember talking with her last Sunday.

"He plays a mean sax, among other things. Great in bed. Me too. Just ask him." She laughed, but there was no humor in it. "We were having a wonderful time while Daddy got killed. Great timing. But you wouldn't get it."

"Maybe I would," Marti said.

Belle looked at her, then raised her drink in a toast. "So, you know. Smart cop. Who told you? Or are Denise and I so obviously screwed up that you just guessed?" She sipped her drink. "Funny, isn't it? He was good to Terri and she's more screwed up than both of us."

Didn't they think Terri had been molested too?

"Did you check Terri's alibi?" Belle asked. "I know how pregnant she is, but don't let that helpless act fool you. She's got a key to the place, which is more than he ever gave me, even when I lived there."

Had Hamilton given a key to anyone else? Did Gladys know Terri had a key?

"Terri hated him. Her own daddy and she hated him. He spoiled her. That's why. People don't appreciate you when you give them everything they want before they even get a chance to ask for it. Dolls, clothes, toys, ballet lessons, piano. I had to teach myself. You name it, Terri got it. He sure as hell never spoiled me.

"My daddy, my daddy," she mimicked. "If you

are thinking that one of us did it, don't look to Denise. She's all the mother I ever had. She ain't got it in her to hurt nobody. You look to Terri if you've got to look at one of us."

"Why?"

"Miss Goody Two-Shoes, Terri." Belle went on as if Marti hadn't spoken. "That conniving little liar. I took more whippings for what she did than for anything I ever did myself. She hated him. She took him to a faith healer when he found those lumps in his stomach. Know why? A doctor might have gotten them out in time, so it couldn't spread." Belle leaned across the table. "Zaar is almost five. That was when he started liking us. You mark my words, Terri got one of those men she sneaks around and sleeps with to kill the old fool. She got jealous because Daddy was asking her to bring Zaar over. She's been in a snit over that and acting crazy for weeks."

With that, Belle tossed off her drink and got up. "You think it's one of us? Look at Terri. And leave Denise alone. She's gone through enough. I don't appreciate nobody messing with Denise. She's good people. Loves me more than my momma." She reached for her coat. "I'll tell the boyfriend we're through talking."

"Did you get what you came for?" Ben asked when he came in.

"I might have got more."

"You don't seem too happy about it."

"I just want to close this damned case."

"Ready to go?"

She shook her head.

"This might be a good show. You should have heard her at the funeral."

Marti positioned herself so that she could see the stage and keep an eye on the front door.

By eight o'clock a dozen people were scattered about the room and a skinny girl in a miniskirt and a halter with a towel tied around her waist was serving drinks. Belle's hips swayed as she made her way to the stage, but she didn't stagger. As soon as she sat at the piano, the talking stopped.

"I've got a friend with me tonight who's great on the cello so I asked her sit in with me for a few songs . . . Jolene Cooper."

The woman who had come in with Belle walked to the stage and set up the cello. A few people applauded.

Belle began with "The First Time Ever I Saw Your Face." Marti rubbed her finger against the initials carved into the table and remembered the way Johnny would smooth back her hair and whisper "sweet thing" in her ear.

Belle sang half a dozen ballads accompanied by the cellist. Her voice captured every nuance of emotion as she took everyone in the room exactly where she wanted them to go. As Belle leaned back, eyes closed, and sang, "Just Like a

Woman," Marti realized she was holding Ben's hand, tightly. She didn't let go.

For the next hour and half, Belle took her meager audience through a repertoire that included blues, jazz, oldies, and soul.

Belle concluded with a wild and sensual dance with the saxophone player to "I Wanna Dance with Somebody."

Then, leaning heavily on the sax player's arm, she left the stage. She had taken only two breaks, but the waitress had kept the drinks coming. "Be back in half an hour," Belle said, speech slurred.

"Not likely," a man in the next booth said. "Show's over."

When they got in the car, Ben leaned his head against the back of the seat and said, "Wow. Who would believe it?"

"I know," Marti agreed. Such an incredible voice, and so few people to hear it. "I wonder . . . ," she began, but didn't finish the thought aloud. What if Gladys had never met Henry Hamilton at all? What if Belle and Denise . . . ?

Ben reached across the seat and brushed a stray curl away from her face.

A half hour after Marti got home she got a call that someone had spotted a floater. When the body was pulled from the Des Plaines River, it turned out to be men's clothing stuffed with straw, something left over from Halloween.

C H A P T E R
28

When Belle woke up she could see light around the edges of the window shade. She was alone, on the couch. Had she sent sweet Eddie away? She couldn't remember, but she had wanted him to stay. She closed her eyes. Her mouth tasted like she had vomited. At least her head didn't hurt much. She should get up, find something to drink, get this taste out of her mouth. She should. She felt along the floor as far as her arm could reach, found the bottle of scotch. Empty. She sat up on one elbow, drank the last few drops.

That cop came to the club last night and she told her about Terri. Maybe now Little Miss Innocence would get a little more attention from the police. There wasn't anything that sneaky, lying heifer wouldn't do. Momma's girl, Daddy's girl. Lying whore, that's what, using her pregnancies to hold everyone's attention just like she used her dancing and lousy piano playing when she was a kid. Little Miss Spotlight.

Sickly Terri, never well enough to help around the house, never sick enough to stay inside and not go out to play, or dance, or find some boy to screw. Terri who lived with the dead. Did Terri visit him, down there in the basement? Momma wasn't there to get in the way.

Momma. How could that woman not know what he did to her and Denise? So what if she was at church all the time. At least Momma had someplace to go to get away from him. Woman gave years of her life to that church and left her and Denise with him. Why couldn't she see? Wasn't there some mother's instinct or intuition that told her something was wrong? Maybe she did know, and just didn't care.

She wouldn't be a mother, ever. Wouldn't bring nobody into this world for someone else to hurt. She didn't have to worry about sweet Eddie or nobody else messing with no child of hers. Wouldn't ever have to raise nobody, look out for nobody, feed nobody but herself. It was good, just having herself to look after. She wouldn't have been any better at looking after a kid than Momma was. And no better at picking out a daddy.

Henry Hamilton. Daddy. The first time she ever saw him she thought he was the tallest, handsomest man she had ever seen. She had been so happy when Momma brought him home, when he let her sit on his lap, when he brought her and Denise those walking dolls, the first dolls they had ever seen with brown faces. She thought he would love them. She wanted to love him. She did love him, until he hurt her.

She wouldn't have been mean to him like Terri was if he had loved her the way he loved Terri. She would have taken him right to the doctor when he got sick, made him find out what was wrong those times he went to the emergency room. They didn't care, Momma and Terri. They liked seeing him sickly and weak. She would have loved him, if he had let her. Why couldn't he love them all, be kind to them all the way he was to Terri? Was it that important that Terri was his own child and they weren't?

Did Terri kill him? Poor Terri, everyone said. They didn't know that Terri stole money from him, that she lied like some people breathed. That she'd been fooling around with boys since fifth grade. That she was sleeping with old man Ezra's cousin's kid and that it was probably his baby, not Ezra's, that she was carrying now. Nobody knew. Terri fooled everyone. Sweet little Terri, that's what everyone thought. She lost her daddy. They should say poor Belle, because she had loved him. The old man had loved Terri and used her and Denise. But she had loved him, long ago.

Her head was beginning to hurt. What day was it? Sunday. She put her hand to her forehead. She hoped she had some Tylenol to tide her over until she could get a drink.

CHAPTER
29

Marti was at her desk munching cold pizza when Vik arrived at the precinct Sunday evening. She had slept in this morning, gone to second service for the first time in over a month. Afterward she and the kids had gone out to lunch, then ice-skating at a local rink. Spending the day with her family had been great.

Vik scowled as he draped his coat over the back of his chair.

"You did take the afternoon off, right, Jessenovik?"

"Mildred and I went to breakfast after Mass."

"And?"

"I canvassed the neighborhood again."

"Vik!"

"Sunday seemed like a good day."

"You're becoming a workaholic."

"What else is new?" He checked the coffeepot

and looked disappointed. "Cowboy hasn't been in today." He made the coffee.

"Did you come up with anything else?" Marti asked.

"Somebody walking a dog, maybe one-thirty or two. No description of either. The guy who saw this was a real youngster, not more than sixty-five."

Vik took a piece of pizza and made a face before he bit into cold pepperoni. "We haven't reached a dead end on this one, MacAlister. We've just got too many suspects, too little information, and alibis for the wrong people."

He took out a blank piece of paper and a ruler and began drawing a grid. "Why would anyone in their right mind want to molest kids?"

"They're helpless," Marti said. "And it's hard to say no to an adult when you're little. And adults are always right. And . . ."

"I know," he said sharply, and added a few choice Polish invectives. Then he glanced at Marti, remembered that she could translate, and shut up.

After filling in the blocks he'd drawn, Vik said, "I've listed the suspects—Gladys, Denise, Danzel, Vera, Belle, Terri, Vera's sister, Sissy, and unknown."

She would have organized them that way, too, from most to least likely, with Danzel's ranking based on Vik's certainty that Gladys was lying.

"And I've indicated opportunity or alibi. Vera says she and her little girl spent the night with her sister, so they're alibis for each other. If Danzel's lady friend is lying, she might reconsider before it went to court. Motive is our weakest link. Nobody seems to have one that's strong enough to justify killing him when they did. Even if Denise was there, and we haven't proved that to my satisfaction, I don't think possible abuse thirty years ago constitutes a motive."

"No," Marti agreed. "Whatever precipitated this was much more recent than that. The only thing that I've come up with is an arguement Gladys and Henry might have had at church. If we haven't made an arrest by Wednesday, I'm going to check out the next deacons' meeting."

"Considering what Hamilton's done, Marti, it would be a damned shame to have to bring any of these women in. Hard to believe, isn't it? What did he say to himself? 'Well, Vera will be seven next Thursday, time to move on to Sissy'?" Vik shook his head. "I don't understand. If he were a young man, we could blame it on drugs. But this guy was recruiting these kids through his church. And the way our list of suspects is shaping up, when we do arrest someone, I'm going to feel like apologizing for bringing her in."

"Maybe there will be some kind of extenuating circumstance," Marti said. But not if they found out that same someone systematically had been trying to poison him as well. She didn't mention that possibility. It was too tenuous until the autopsy reports came in, something to keep in the back of her mind.

"He was sleeping when they got him," Vik said. "Not much provocation in that. And if it does have anything to do with abuse, so much time has passed that it'll just look premeditated."

Marti thought of the children, Zaar and Tiffany. Was someone trying to protect them? They were close to the age of Terri and Vera when it happened to them. "Not much we can do about that," was all she said.

There was a knock on the door. Marti looked up and saw Howie Sikich. What did he want?

"Lieutenant Videlko called in with the flu," he said. "And Lieutenant Dirkowitz is out all week at the seminar."

Marti turned to Vik. Lieutenant Sikich was two years younger than he was. He handled procurement and other administrative responsibilities. He had nothing to do with investigations or any other police activity. Was Sikich third in command?

Standing, the top of Sikich's head just came to her shoulder. Sikich pulled up a chair and straddled it. "I need a complete briefing on the Hamilton case, immediately. I expect all of your reports typed, signed, and on my desk by seven each morning."

Vik stood up. "Sure thing, but the briefing will have to wait. We don't have that kind of time to waste right now."

Sikich nodded while Vik was speaking, then said nothing, as if he hadn't understood any of it.

"Marti and I are just leaving," Vik told him. "This will have to wait."

"I'm the officer in charge now."

"No, sir," Vik corrected. "We are the officers in charge of this investigation. You are the officer we report to. We cannot report to you now because we cannot interrupt our investigation."

Sikich stopped nodding and looked at the pizza. "You seem to have found time to eat."

"While we were working, sir. And now we're leaving." He took another bite of the pizza slice and threw away the rest.

Marti grabbed her coat and hurried to catch up with Vik. Downstairs, Vik stopped to talk to the sergeant. "Do me a favor, he said. His finger jabbed the air. "Keep Sikich the hell out of my way."

The sergeant shrugged. "We try harder."

"Do it," Vik said. "Or we'll have a homicide inside the precinct. Manual strangulation."

"Sounds good to me," the sergeant said.

Vik didn't speak again until they were in the car. As he fumed quietly, Marti said, "I suppose I get to find out why nobody likes him."

"I don't know who in the hell his chinaman is, but if I ever get my hands on the son of . . ."

Marti wondered about Sikich's chinaman, too. She'd heard that in New York they called a cop's mentor and protector a rabbi. "What's the problem? How do we deal with him?"

Vik took several deep breaths, swore again. "The man doesn't function in the real world. The best way to deal with him is with an AK-47."

"Why do they call him Little Howie behind his back?" she asked. "His name isn't even Howard, it's Francis."

"Because he's an ass. Before he got that desk job he drove for Chief Howard."

"Howard's been retired almost twenty years. Drove for him? With his rank?"

"Sikich drove for Howard because after four years of ineptitude, nobody knew what else to do with him. Finally he screwed up on a homicide investigation. The perp walked and six months later he raped and killed another sixteen-year-old boy in California."

"And they kept him on the force?"

"His grandfather was the mayor of Lincoln Prairie half a hundred years ago. His father was an alderman, had a lot of cronies. My father used to call them the Croatian mafia. They had enough clout to get him that desk job he's had the last nineteen years."

"In charge of procurement?" She tried to avoid

at least some of the office gossip. "Is he the reason we ran out of toilet paper in September?"

"You got it."

"And we have more incompetence to look forward to."

"Maybe we'll get lucky and he'll go away or get sick before I kill him. Lieutenant Videlko shouldn't be out long. The flu only lasts a couple of days."

"Usually."

She drove to a nearby Dunkin' Donuts and they sat in the parking lot for twenty minutes with the engine running, sipping coffee, and eating chocolate cream-filleds while she told him about her trip to see Belle the night before.

"Danzel does seem like quite the ladies' man," she said. "Maybe Terri does have a boyfriend and he's it. It would be convenient."

"I don't know how we'll find out," Vik said.

"This is the first we've heard of Terri playing around, and it sounded like jealousy. Terri seems to think every man in the world can't wait to get his hands on her, but I can't imagine her turning anyone on while she's pregnant. Denise is right. She looks terminally ill."

"I can't get a good feel for this one," Vik admitted. "The most logical suspects are still his family. But even if it was someone else, something had to trigger it."

"Hamilton had been sick. And a lot of people

think that suffocation looks like natural causes," Marti said. "Someone stops breathing. They don't realize that we can identify it. Everyone knew he was sick. Even that might have been deliberately induced." She thought for a minute. "If we do identify a poisonous substance he ingested, that would point to Gladys. She ate with him every day but didn't get sick."

"Well, it doesn't look like anyone is going to confess, so I guess we're going to have to solve this the old-fashioned way," Vik said. "With a lot more legwork and a preponderance of evidence."

Marti felt like stretching her legs but didn't want to get out of the car. If it wasn't for Sikich they'd be at the precinct. "If Lieutenant Videlko doesn't get over the flu real quick, it could be a long week."

No way was she going to let Sikich run them out of their office again.

C H A P T E R
30

Monday morning, Marti couldn't find a space in the parking lot near the entrance to the precinct. Despite overcast skies, she whistled as the wind almost pushed her along. Theo, who until now had exhibited little interest in athletics, had found out last night that he made the park district basketball team. This morning, Joanna had shown her a report that she had completed for the class she liked the least, biology. She had brought a D in that subject up to a B. Marti hadn't seen enough of the kids in the past few weeks to have contributed much to their success, but instead of guilt as usual, she had a feeling of impending maturity. Theirs.

When she went upstairs, the officer who had the cubicle across from her office was packing personal belongings into boxes.

"Look's like Traffic's moving," she told Vik as

she hung up her coat. "Who gave them the green light? I don't remember hearing anything about relocations." Her in-basket was overflowing with routine interoffice mail. "We generate enough memos around here to kill off a forest in a year." She scanned one. " 'Snow route parking is now in effect in the event of snow.' Real motivational. I think I'll read the others next week."

She checked the blue ceramic mug Joanna had made. "Ugh. I think that's mold."

She wiped it out with a handful of tissues, then held the mug toward Vik. "What do you think? Do I have to wash it?"

Vik didn't answer. He didn't even grunt in response. His eyebrows were almost meeting across the bridge of his nose. "Command post," he said.

"Huh?"

"Traffic is moving temporarily because Sikich is establishing a command post."

"Right outside our door?" She closed it.

"Maybe we can start keeping the coffeepot in the closet," Vik said. "So far he's had two cups, used the pencil sharpener, and borrowed a box of paper clips. I think he wanted to know where you were and didn't have enough nerve to ask."

She felt good this morning. Sikich was not going to intrude. "What the hell, Vik. This is probably the most exciting thing that's happened to Little Howie in the last ten years. Ordering toilet paper can't be much fun. Let him have his little command post. Just keep him there."

"MacAlister, we're not looking for a mass murderer or a serial killer here. What kind of a command post do you need to arrest somebody who wields a pillow?"

"Oh, Vik, come on. Look on the bright side. This is temporary.

"Right. And maybe he'll call in a swat team when we're ready to apprehend the perp. We haven't done anything like that since you've been here."

Vik organized a folder full of typed forms. "Got your notes together?"

"For what?"

"We meet with Sikich at eight-fifteen."

"I thought our meeting was right after roll call. I was hoping I'd miss it because I had to pick up some reports."

"He moved it up twice because you weren't here."

Marti half-filled a foam cup with coffee. She didn't have enough time to wash her mug. "Well, he'd better make it fast. I want to get over to Dolly Patterson's house by nine."

"Sikich comes first. Let's see what kind of a mood you're in when you're finished with him. Show me the reports you wrote up over the weekend."

She tore off five sheets of handwritten notes

from a yellow legal pad and found the forms she'd filled in by hand.

Vik almost smiled as he scanned them. "We don't want him to know you can type?"

"Nah."

He made a noise that came close to a chuckle. "And you don't think in complete sentences either. This is great. When we give this to Sikich, I'll put my notes on top. We'll dazzle him with brilliance, then baffle him with bullshit."

"Suppose he wants our files?"

"Let's let him think of that. Maybe he won't."

"How's Videlko feeling?" she asked.

"It's not the twenty-four-hour flu. He'll be out for at least another day."

"Too bad. I don't know how much of Sikich I can put up with. How's Lieutenant Dirkowitz on insubordination?"

"He'd expect us to be more creative," Vik said, leaving the room.

When Vik returned with the copies of their notes he shook his head. "He's having two phones installed so that he can coordinate field operations."

"Is that us? Are we both supposed to call in at the same time?"

"Look, MacAlister, please do not give this idiot any ideas." He tore out the third page of the autopsy report, crumpled it and tossed it into the wastebasket, then changed the sequence of her handwritten notes. "I think page five here should be page three." He penciled in the page change. "And I forgot how to make those duplex copies. I don't think all of the backs of my reports match the fronts."

Vik smiled as he put everything into a folder. "This ought to keep him busy for the rest of the day. The one thing we've got going for us is that it takes this guy half an hour to decide if he wants his coffee black or with creamer. Even when he was functioning as a cop he couldn't remember police procedure long enough to make an arrest stick. Things have changed so much since then that he probably won't even be able to interpret the language. Nickel bet we don't hear from him again until tomorrow."

As Marti drove over to see Gladys's sister, unannounced, tiny snowflakes hit the windshield and disappeared. This little hint of snow was just a reminder that winter was coming. There wouldn't be enough to cover the ground. Vik wouldn't be too happy with the weather, out canvassing again.

Dolly Patterson lived in a subdivision near the golf course. The streets were narrow and tree-lined. Her house, a brick trilevel, was half hidden by a privacy fence. Dolly was a plumper version of Gladys, with the same coppery skin and the same deep-set eyes and high cheekbones.

She was several years older than her sister, but she looked younger and smiled easily. There was a hint of laughter or mischief in her eyes.

Dolly's kitchen was as modern as Gladys's was antiquated and as cheerful as Marti's own, with orange, gold, and yellow wallpaper and an herb garden on a plant stand near a wide window. A fat black-and-white cat was sunning itself on the windowsill.

"Do you garden too?" Marti asked.

"Yes, but for pleasure. I don't can or freeze a thing. Give away whatever I can't eat. There's nothing in the world that tastes better than a fresh-picked tomato. And poke salad. I grow that and mustard greens from my own seeds every year."

Marti declined an offer of coffee—one cup of her own was enough to last until noon—but accepted a glass of orange juice.

"I'm surprised you didn't come sooner."

Marti didn't reply.

"I've given this a lot of thought. What to say, what not to say. Whether or not to say anything at all."

Mrs. Patterson looked out the window for a few minutes, watching as the cat flicked its tail twice and closed its eyes.

"I want you to understand about Gladys. She's the youngest, the baby, six years younger than me. We had two older brothers, but they're both gone now. They say Mother was real happy when she had me, that she always wanted a girl. I can remember helping Mother roll out Christmas cookies when I was five. There's just the two of us, Mother would say. She didn't expect to have any more children. The doctor told her that she had a tipped womb and couldn't get pregnant again. Then, there I was going to school and along came Gladys. I think if we were closer in age it would have been easier for Mother to accept."

Dolly looked out the window for a while, watched the cat sleep.

"I'm not sure Gladys ever did anything that quite pleased Mother. I'm not sure she ever could, and she was smart enough not to keep trying for too long. Then, when she had Denise and Belle, that justified every complaint and criticism Mother ever had. Too bad Joe Nathan was already married. Just being with him made Gladys happy. When Gladys married Henry, Mother wasn't too pleased at first. All of a sudden Gladys was doing everything Mother always said she wanted her to and Mother couldn't find fault. But you see, when Gladys married Henry, it was like living with Mother again. He was always real critical of her. Even when they were courting, although that didn't last long, he made her change her hairstyle and he all but forbid her to buy a hat. Said it was vanity. Me and Denise bought her one every chance we got, she loves them so much. There wasn't anything he could say about that. They say you marry your parent, become like your mother eventually. I did. And so did Gladys. She's just like mother now. We are each like the mother we knew."

Dolly emptied her glass. "More juice?"

Marti shook her head. Dolly poured more for herself.

"After my husband died I asked Gladys if she'd stay with me on the weekends, not because I'm lonely, but to get her out of the house and away from him for a while."

"Why?"

"To see her smile again, make her laugh, treat her to some little pleasure that Henry wouldn't allow. I always did that when we were children together. Henry couldn't stand me, and he didn't want her over here, but I told him I'd go to Reverend Douglas and tell him how selfish he was being, denying me the companionship of my sister during my bereavement. I've been widowed five years now. After a while Gladys's coming here became like a habit."

"The two of you went shopping the day Henry died."

"Henry must have had some kind of premonition. He actually let her use a credit card for the first time."

"Could he have been making up to her for an argument, maybe?"

"Argue? Gladys and Henry? It takes two. Gladys stopped talking back years ago."

"Henry could just say whatever he wanted?"

"Henry thought he was perfect. He never did anything wrong, so of course he could be critical of everyone else. If he threw something in Gladys's face, there wasn't anything she could say back. I know it sounds mean-spirited, but I often wonder if he didn't marry her so he'd have someone to look down on. He actually told me that I wasn't a fit wife because my husband fixed his own lunch. Gladys had to prepare all of his meals, even when she spent the night here. And he was so petty. Take that pokeweed. Gladys loved it, but she didn't care much for collards. So guess what grew in his garden? She had to pick some of mine."

The cat woke up, eyed them without interest, stretched, and jumped to the floor.

"If you had come here the day before yesterday, I wouldn't have told you anything. I had to be sure in my own heart that Gladys didn't put that pillow on his face. Lord knows that man gave her enough cause to. But she is my sister. I've known her longer and loved her more than anyone else in this world, and I'm satisfied, in my own mind, that she didn't do it. That's why I've told you all this."

Marti looked down at her half-filled glass of

orange juice. Joe Nathan also knew Gladys pretty well, and he didn't think she did it either.

When Marti returned to her desk, she put in a call to the Botanical Gardens in Glencoe. Momma cooked something called poke salad. She wanted to be certain it was the same thing.

Vik looked up from the reports he was scanning when she hung up. "What was that all about?"

"Dolly grows a wild weed that's kind of like dandelions. Some people call it wild spinach because that's what it looks like. Dolly called it Pokeweed. My mother called it poke salad."

"And?"

"It grows wild in the South and every part of it is poisonous—root, stem, leaf, berry."

Vik considered that for a minute. "People pick something that's poisonous and eat it? On purpose?"

"Right. They pick the leaves, boil them, and pour off the water. That gets rid of the poison. My mother cooked them with collard and mustard greens and salt pork. I've eaten them. They taste good."

"I wonder how many people died before they figured how to cook them."

"The things you think of," Marti said.

She called the coroner's office. "Janet says there would be traces of it in Hamilton's tissue and blood samples. She's going to have them test for it. It'll take at least another week."

"It's a good thing we're not trying to determine what killed him."

"No, but we are trying to figure out who did it." She thought about that. "Henry was a big man. From what we know, Gladys didn't stand up to him. This would be sneaky, something an intimidated person might get a lot of satisfaction from."

"MacAlister, we're having enough problems with this one. Don't go off on a tangent."

"If it comes down to a choice of suspects, this could be what tips the balance. Something over the past year and a half made Henry become sickly and weak. If someone had tried to put a pillow over his head before then, he would have given them quite a fight. I don't think they would have succeeded."

Vik had no answer for that.

A little before five a tall, willowy blond woman came in.

"Yes?" Marti said.

The woman extended her hand. "Laura Spencer."

"Detective MacAlister."

"I'm an investigator with the Fidelity Mutual Insurance Company."

"Have a seat," Vik offered. "What can we do for you?"

"We have a policy on Henry Hamilton. I understand you're investigating his death."

Marti didn't remember the name of the company Gladys's insurance policy on Henry was with, but Vik did, and she could tell by his expression that it wasn't Fidelity Mutual.

"Who's the beneficiary?" Vik asked.

"His daughter, Terri Whittaker. She inquired about cashing in the policy this morning and told us the cause of death was suffocation. We said it would take a few days to release the check, but we can't, obviously, until you've completed your investigation."

"What's the face value?"

"Fifty thousand."

Marti and Vik answered a few questions without telling Ms. Spencer anything about the investigation, and agreed to get back to her when they'd made an arrest.

"I think we want to talk with Danzel Whittaker again," Vik said. "Let's surprise him."

"Let's find out where he is."

The elder Mrs. Whittaker answered the phone. Marti didn't identify herself. No need to alert Danzel.

"He's on his way to East St. Louis to deliver a body and will probably stay overnight," Marti said.

Vik consulted his notes. "He drives a red Trans Am. Let's have the black-and-white that patrols the funeral home beat see if it's there. If not, we can have him keep an eye out for it and alert the unit that patrols where the girlfriend lives as well. Fifty thousand dollars sounds like a damned good motive to me."

C H A P T E R
31

Marti felt as cranky as Vik looked when she got to work Tuesday morning. Sikich was standing at the entrance to his command post. Marti went into the office without speaking to him and closed the door.

"Looks like Little Howie figured out those reports we gave him yesterday," she said.

"Yeah, but it took him all day. He's read last night's reports too. He's real agitated this morning. Keeps popping his head in looking for you. You're going to have to stop disappearing after roll call. The man's had open heart surgery. We probably don't really want him to have another heart attack."

"Don't be too sure about that."

She looked at the folders stacked on her desk, her overflowing in-basket, the report forms she had to complete. She picked up her mug, then put it down. She had forgotten to rinse it out again. "We've got court this afternoon. Let's just get this over with. His place or ours?"

Vik went to the door and invited Sikich in. Little Howie brought their reports with him, along with several folders, and sat at Slim's desk, which was much neater than Cowboy's. "I've read through these reports. I have indicated the action you are to take in red pen in the margins. I have also indicated in blue pencil anything that I do not agree with or feel you should take corrective action on."

Vik's jaws tightened. Marti resisted a strong urge to lift Sikich from the chair and slap him. She didn't have the time or the patience to train him and he definitely was not going to tell them how to conduct an investigation.

"And MacAlister, your reports will have to be typed from now on."

"Takes time, sir. You want them ASAP."

He looked at her for a few moments, then said, "I don't suppose you can type very fast?"

"It's not in my job description, sir."

"Well, I do have to have these reports on a timely basis," he conceded.

Vik relaxed, raising one eyebrow. Marti suppressed a smile.

"Now, what I fail to understand is why Gladys Hamilton and Denise Stevens have not been brought in for questioning. It's very obvious from these reports that they're serious suspects, but I don't see any pressure being brought to bear to get a confession. I want that rectified immediately. I expect to see them both brought in for questioning today."

Marti looked at Vik. "Sir, we don't operate that way," he said. "We conduct an investigation. When there is a preponderance of evidence, when we are satisfied as to method, motive, and opportunity, then we question the suspect, unless we have some logical reason to otherwise harass and annoy them."

"You have two suspects, Jessenovik. They are the only possible suspects. These reports indicate a history of sexual abuse. That is certainly sufficient motive. I think you're putting this off because of Denise's position within the department. We cannot play favoritism here."

"People play favorites all the time, sir," Vik said quietly. "Sometimes with the help of a chinaman."

Red-faced, Sikich brought down his fist on the desk. "There is no reason whatsoever to drag your feet on this. I want an arrest made today."

"So do I, sir," Vik said, speaking softly. "But there won't be one. First, there is no preponderance of evidence. We have indications, sir, indications that some type of abuse might have existed. Maybe. We have nothing other than people's word to substantiate it."

Sikich slammed his fist on the desk again. "It is substantiated."

"There are no witnesses to confirm that Hamilton abused any member of his family. He had an alleged preference for five-to-seven-year-old females. His daughter and his stepdaughters are all adults now, and none are living at home."

"Jessenovik!" Sikich yelled. "I will not tolerate this double-talk and procrastination. I want an arrest today! Get both of those women in here!"

Slowly, Vik got to his feet and put both hands on the desk where Sikich sat. "With all due respect, sir, we have an excellent arrest record. We have managed to achieve this without falsely accusing or erroneously arresting anyone. We are police officers, sir. This is not the gestapo. When we have enough evidence to take to the state's attorney, and when we are convinced we have the right suspect, we will take immediate and appropriate action. If you want to be a hanging committee of one, that's your business. But you'll have to wait for the next homicide and work on that case by yourself. We will not engage in or take responsibility for sloppy, inept police work."

Marti felt like applauding. She had never seen Vik this angry. Sikich looked up at Vik, speechless. He gathered the papers he'd brought in and slammed the door as he left.

"Stupid," Vik said.

They worked in silence for about twenty minutes. The sleet had shifted to rain and the flag on the pole just outside their window was unfurled and blowing almost straight out.

"Nice day to stay inside," Marti said.

Vik didn't answer.

"As far as we know, Jessenovik, Danzel is still in East St. Louis. His car is still parked behind Whittaker's Funeral Home. Since we can't prove any unusual connection between him and Terri, let's talk to Ezra. Maybe we can shake the tree a little bit."

Ezra agreed to come in. For some reason he looked even older today. The stoop of his shoulders was more pronounced, and there were dark pouches under his eyes. His hairline was receding, and his white hair was so thin that Marti could see his scalp. Like Belle, Terri seemed to have a preference for fair-skinned men, but Ezra didn't have Henry Hamilton's height.

"How's Terri?" Marti asked, trying not to think of husband and wife together in bed. These May—December marriages always puzzled her. She could never quite buy into the younger partner being head over heels in love.

"Now that the wake and funeral are over she's feeling much better. She was quite close to her father."

Close enough to marry someone almost his age, Marti thought.

"I know these relationships often seem unusual to outsiders, but she's a good wife and we're very happy together." It sounded like something he had said before.

"Of course, sometimes it's hard for an old man like me to keep up with her, but so far I've managed." He grinned in a way that seemed self-congratulatory.

"It is a little difficult, at my age, to start a family, but Zaar is a sweet little girl. Terri has such a difficult time with her pregnancies that I'm hoping she won't want to try again. But that's her decision, and if she insists . . ." He grinned again.

"So, how can I help you? I've got two funerals in the next three days. I need to get back as soon as possible."

"You can tell me what Terri did during the two weeks before her father died. Where she went, with whom, and when."

He seemed concerned by the question. "To the doctor. Danzel drove. That's it. She doesn't even shop anymore."

"And last Friday night?"

"She wanted to go shopping for the new baby, but just wasn't up to it. I didn't have a viewing until Saturday morning, so we spent the evening together."

"And that night?"

"That's getting a bit personal. We do sleep in the same bed, ordinarily, but she's been so uncomfortable lately that she's been sleeping alone."

"Could she leave the house at night without your knowing it?"

"No. She would have to pass the room I'm sleeping in and my mother's room as well. We've been leaving our doors open in case of an emergency."

"And Terri was home that night?"

"Yes. You can't be implying that Terri would harm her own father?"

Vik took over.

"Is Terri the beneficiary of a fifty-thousand-dollar insurance policy on the life of her father?"

"What?" There was nothing feigned in his surprise. "Of course not. She would have told me."

Marti heard the doubt in his voice.

"Terri would have told me about something like that."

"Then there is no policy?"

"No. I'm sure of it."

They both made no mention of Danzel. Vik stood up. "We're due in court in about half an hour. We'll call if we have any further questions."

"Thanks for coming in," Marti said.

As self-assured as he had been when he came in, Ezra seemed a bit preoccupied when he left.

CHAPTER
32

Denise left work on time Tuesday night so she could go over to Momma's and pick up the rest of the old man's belongings, things in the basement that Momma had forgotten about. As she walked down the hall to his room she felt that same sense of fear and revulsion that she had known as a child. It had never left her, not even as an adult.

His clothes were stacked at the foot of the bed. Stomach churning, she stood there, staring at the place where his head had been before they took him away. For so many nights, while Momma was at church, she had come trembling with dread to this room, stomach churning. She had sat on his lap in that old horsehair chair dispatched to the city dump years ago. She would stiffen against him as his hands began rubbing the inside of her thighs, and the more rigid she became, the more that pleased him. He wanted her to be afraid. For a long time he just rubbed her, slowly at first, then faster and faster until he was panting, then stopped all at once.

That March when she turned six, it changed. He let her see it, watch it grow while he rubbed her. In her dreams it was larger than she was, no longer a part of him but something unto itself, towering over her, covering her, drowning her. And when she woke crying for Momma, she could not say what she had dreamed.

Next, he pushed her head down to where it was, rubbing her, making her face feel sticky and wet. "Your mouth, girl," he urged her, laughing when she didn't understand, forcing her head down with a hand on her neck.

Then, in March, she turned seven and he sent for Belle instead. She felt such relief. It was only when Belle had stopped trying to make her laugh and she saw Belle wasn't laughing anymore either that she had stopped feeling glad. Momma noticed too, then said with a sigh, "I can't remember being like that myself, Henry, but Denise got quiet too when she turned five. Maybe it's just a phase. Have you noticed how Denise's appetite's been picking up these past few weeks? She'll be something more than skin and bones again soon. As fat as she was as a baby, she's gone down to nearly nothing these past few years."

She had been scared to go to him and be touched, scared that what she swallowed would make her sick or kill her, scared that Momma wouldn't love her if she knew.

And Belle, laughing Belle, with all the laughter gone.

"Hellish," Momma said when Belle was bad at school, or acted up at church, or got into fights in the neighborhood. "Devil's sure got into her." Neither belt nor switch beat the devil out of Belle, but Belle did become clever in her mischief. More often it looked accidental, couldn't be helped, couldn't be punished.

One night, she and Belle kept looking at each other. They just sat on their beds looking across the room at each other until the tears came to their eyes and ran down their faces. They sat there, crying without making any noise, not saying anything, until they both wiped away their tears and Denise turned out the lights.

The next time he sent for Belle, Denise went instead. He never said a word. He sat her on it. The pain got so bad she thought he was ripping her open. He held his handkerchief over her mouth. There was blood. She didn't know if she would stop bleeding.

Afterward, Belle stood by her bed and looked at her, eyes wide, afraid, wanting to know what he did and not wanting to find out, grateful that he hadn't done it to her. Denise's stomach hurt for three days. She threw up everything, even water. Momma thought she had the flu, and she stayed in bed for a week.

When she was better and back in school and Tuesday night came again, Momma put on her second-best hat and went to Bible study. He sent for Belle. The two of them stood stock-still in the kitchen listening to his voice, hearing the annoyance when Belle didn't go to him at once and he had to call her name again. They looked at each other and held hands. Belle gave Denise's hand a little squeeze and went down the hall without looking back.

Now he was dead. She wanted to throw back her head and laugh but, like Belle, she had no laughter left. She had nothing but this emptiness inside that could never be healed or even soothed by time. It was too late for his death to matter to her or Belle at all.

C H A P T E R
33

At roll call Wednesday morning, the sergeant announced that Lieutenant Videlko would not be returning to work until the following Monday. "I suggested that he might want to come in on Friday, before Lieutenant Dirkowitz gets back, just to have the opportunity to work with Lincoln Prairie's own Dyspeptic and Dynamic Duo. He said he's itching to see what Jessenovik and Mac-Alister have been up to since things have been a little slow in the arrest department, but the doctor says no."

Everyone laughed except Sikich. He left without hearing the rest of the announcements. Vik grinned and flashed her a V sign. Marti felt depressed. Four more days of Sikich. She didn't realize how much she loathed coming to work and dealing with him every morning until she thought of Lieutenant Dirkowitz's return on Monday.

Upstairs, Slim commiserated. "Another four days before our resident idiot goes back to issuing purchase orders."

Cowboy measured coffee. "It might be prudent to suggest to someone that this third-in-command situation be remedied. Some people shouldn't be allowed to have a responsible position within the law enforcement community."

"Some people shouldn't be allowed inside a precinct," Vik said, closing the door. "You two might be able to help us with something."

Marti rummaged around in her top drawer until she found a Hershey's bar she'd been saving for an energy crisis. She really did feel depressed, an uncommon emotion for her. Maybe some chocolate would help.

Before she could unwrap the candy bar, the door was pushed open with such force that the knob banged against the wall. Sikich stood in the doorway waving their reports in the air. "This . . . this . . ." he sputtered. "Why hasn't an arrest been made yet? You've got all you need." He took a step into the room. "The two of you are off this case, effective immediately. I am having a warrant issued for Denise Stevens's arrest ASAP. She will be in jail by this afternoon."

"Sir!" Marti felt a rush of anger so immediate that her stomach seemed to ball up in a knot. Vik touched his earlobe, a signal to wait. She expected Vik to protest, but he leaned back in his chair, cradling his coffee cup in both hands. He seemed more pleased than upset.

"And furthermore, I'm citing you both for dereliction of duty."

"Somebody's in a real snit this morning," Slim said. "Maybe you just need a cup of coffee, sir. Sorry it's not ready yet. We're running a little slow this morning. Big night last night. Eleven arrests."

Sikich ignored him, watching Vik. When Vik didn't respond, he said, "By this time tomorrow, neither of you will be Homicide detectives."

"They must have openings in Procurement," Cowboy drawled.

Sikich waited again, unable to provoke any reaction from Vik. Marti looked at Vik. He touched his earlobe again: wait. Why wasn't he upset?

"Furthermore, you will also be written up for insubordination."

"My, my," Slim said. "This might call for Metamucil. Sounds like irregularity to me."

Vik stood and Sikich backed away until he hit the edge of Marti's desk. Vik raised his cup to him, then turned away and filled it with coffee.

Sikich's face turned red as he stared at Vik's back. He waved their reports. "Denise Stevens's car was identified as being at the scene and you've taken no action against her. I'm taking this to the captain this morning. Probable cause.

You've got more than that here and you've done nothing."

Cowboy flexed his muscles and stretched. "If I were you two, I'd start clearing out my desk. As long as this man's been in the department, he knows something we don't."

"Or someone," Slim added.

Sikich glared at the four of them, then stomped out of the room. Glass rattled as he slammed the door.

"That man better watch himself," Slim said. "Remember when he had that bypass surgery last year? They took him out of here on a stretcher. Someone must have told him to cut back on the tantrums. He jumps on one of his clerks every day. The turnover in his department is getting so bad that I went down there one day to talk with this pretty little thing and went back the next and she was gone."

"I suppose ordering toilet paper can be a power trip," Cowboy said. "Imagine what it would be like around here without it."

"Just think back to September," Slim said. "The man can't even do that right. I wonder how long it'll take him to figure out how to get a warrant issued."

Vik picked up the telephone and talked into it with his back turned to them. "Let's go, MacAlister," he said when he hung up.

Slim smiled at him. "I've seen you this way

269

before, Jessenovik. You've been waiting for him to pull something like this, haven't you?

Vik and Marti drove to one of the big brick houses on Sherman Avenue that her kids called mansions. At Christmastime, this one had lights strung from the roof to the evergreen hedges. There was always a nativity scene on one side of the lawn and Santa Claus's entourage on the other. She always drove by with the kids to see the display.

A housekeeper admitted them. The foyer was twice the size of Marti's living room, with a marble floor and a huge chandelier. The artwork caught her attention. She didn't know much about sculptures or paintings, but these looked like originals.

The housekeeper took their coats and led them into a smaller room where half a dozen overstuffed chairs were arranged near a blazing fireplace. An elderly man with thick white hair dozed in front of the fire. An afghan covered his legs.

"That you, Vik?" the man asked without opening his eyes.

"Yes, sir. I brought my partner." Vik nodded to the chairs and Marti sat down.

The man chuckled. "Got stuck with a woman after all." He looked at her with clear, deep blue eyes—the eyes, and the appraising look, of a much younger man. "Not bad," he said, "Sharp, too, from what I hear. Didn't I tell you that you wouldn't get the worst end of the deal?" He smiled at her. "I'm afraid you got that, my dear, but he's a good cop for all of that. Try to make do." Leaning over, he patted her knee lightly.

"So, what brings the two of you here?"

"Sikich is in the process of getting a warrant to arrest Denise Stevens for smothering her step-father."

"Sikich? Videlko is still out with the flu?"

"Yes, sir."

"Sikich. They made a big mistake, allowing him to dispense toilet paper."

The telephone was concealed in a carved mahogany box. The number he called was programmed. "Dan, Little Howie Sikich is trying to get a warrant issued for Denise Stevens. For homicide. Do an old man a favor and stop it for me, will you? And don't be gentle. The man's an ass."

The only Dan that Marti could think of was the state's attorney. And this old man had his direct line.

"Thanks, Dan. How are the kids?"

He listened.

"And the wife? . . . Great . . . I'm sure Patsy will put something together over the holidays. See you then."

Marti was surprised when Vik thanked him and left. She had anticipated more small talk.

"That's it?" she whispered as they waited for the housekeeper to get their coats.

"He knows more about what's happening in the department than we do, MacAlister. And won't tell a thing. He's eighty-seven now. Still sharp and fancies himself a ladies' man. But he falls asleep a lot. He would have been embarrassed if that happened while you were there."

"Are you going to tell me who he is?" Marti said as the front door closed behind them.

"Sikich isn't the only cop around here with a chinaman. And mine's bigger."

"Who is he?"

"John Quinn."

"And?"

"He was state's attorney once, made it as far as lieutenant governor. He was a friend of my father's."

"Is there anyone in this town who you don't know?"

"Probably." He grinned.

"Better watch it, Jessenovik. I think you just set a record for smiling."

When they got back to the precinct, Marti began typing the reports she had given to Sikich in longhand. Things would have to be in order when Lieutenant Dirkowitz got back.

Vik was staring out the window, his mood as

somber as the day. An office pool was circulating on how long they would go without sunshine. Vik had bet on forty-two days. Always the optimist, Marti had picked seventeen, but if they didn't have sunshine by the day after tomorrow she would lose.

They were both waiting for the other shoe to fall, but Sikich was nowhere to be seen. They didn't go near his command post. Everything was quiet. By one o'clock Marti had all of her paperwork in order. Vik got a call from a friend at the *News-Times*. An anonymous caller had tipped them that Denise Stevens was about to be arrested and charged with homicide.

"Sikich," Vik said. "Trying to get even because we stopped that warrant. Sneaky lying . . ."

"Will it be in the paper?"

"No. I had to promise to call as soon as we charge someone, though. And I'll probably get called for a few other favors as well."

CHAPTER

34

It was quarter past six Wednesday night when Denise came to Marti and Vik's office. They had asked her to come after Sikich left for the day.

"We are organizing our lives around that man," Marti complained.

"We are circumventing his efforts to manipulate and control this investigation," Vik countered.

"Right."

Denise was wearing a wide-brimmed black felt hat with an attached scarf that covered her ears and tied under her chin. Her coat was black, too, and flared. She loosened the scarf, took off the coat, and draped it over the back of a chair. She sat down between Marti's desk and Vik's.

They had agreed that Vik would question Denise first, and they would see how she responded.

"We needed more information," Vik said.

Denise didn't look at either of them. She seemed dejected, or maybe just tired. "You think it was someone in the family, and obviously Mother and I are the best suspects. I understand that. And I'm afraid I can't let myself, or maybe you, off the hook. I went out Friday night, alone. I go out alone a lot of nights when I can't sleep. I drive around, find a spot by the lake, watch the water. My favorite place is near Kenosha. That's were I was. Alone. I didn't see anyone, and as far as I know, nobody saw me. I have no alibi."

"Your car was placed around the corner within the window the coroner has given us for time of death."

"I did go to the lake."

"Before or after?"

Denise picked at some imaginary lint on her navy blue suit and said nothing.

"We want to help you," Vik said.

"Yes, I know you do. I appreciate that."

Marti felt frustrated. They did want to help her, but they just didn't know enough of the truth.

Vik fixed Denise a cup of coffee, apologizing because Cowboy had made it three hours earlier. "You're damned good at your job, Stevens. The department needs you." He took out a tin of kolaches that he kept in his file drawer.

Denise took two. It was first time Marti had

seen her eat anything other than carrot sticks. "We are going to have to give up our secrets, aren't we?"

Vik nodded.

"There are those you'll have to pry out of me, those I will not relinquish until I have no choice, those I don't want anyone to ever know."

"We'll try to respect that," Vik said.

Denise ate two more kolaches. "I need time. A day, maybe, to think about it."

"There were others," Marti said.

Denise looked at her, then looked away. Her eyes were moist. "I assumed so. I try to make up for that . . . for what I couldn't do . . . then. He was such a—you want to remember something . . . that was good about growing up. A happy time . . . a time when you weren't afraid. A time when you were just . . . a child." She smiled. It was a bitter, tight smile, filled with memories.

Marti thought about Zaar and Tiffany. "What happens to a woman who was abused when she was five years old when her own daughter turns five?"

"It's often a very difficult time."

"Suppose the abuser is still in their lives, could abuse their daughters too."

Denise looked at Marti for a moment without comprehending, then said, "Terri. Dear God. And I thought she was spoiled."

Marti described what she had observed, told

Denise what Terri had said about men pestering her.

"I'll go over there first thing in the morning and talk with Ezra." She took a deep breath. "I thought Terri was safe. I couldn't protect Belle, I couldn't protect myself . . . can't protect anyone . . . even the children that come to me now. Sometimes they go back . . . sometimes they're hurt again . . . sometimes it seems so futile. But I have to. I have to try.

"I did go out Friday night. I did drive to a spot by the lake near Kenosha. Alone. And I did drive to Momma's, let myself in, and go to his room. I got there about three o'clock. He was already dead."

"Why did you go there?" Vik asked.

"To take his cat."

Vik was too taken aback to say anything.

"He had thrown out all of Momma's hats. You've seen that house. He doesn't let her have anything. No matter what I bring to make things a little easier, a little more pleasant, I never see it again, not even flowers or plants. But her hats—she loves hats. She can spend hours in a store trying them on, picking one out. She must have had twenty or thirty that she kept in the closet in the dining room.

"The first couple of times I took her shopping for one, I never saw them again. Then I got this brilliant idea and asked her, after church services, right in front of Reverend Douglas, where the hat was that she had bought the day before. She was too embarrassed to say anything, but I made a big fuss over it—how much she had enjoyed shopping for it and all. The reverend told her how much his mother had enjoyed a new hat, told her all vanity wasn't wrong."

Denise seemed tired out by the telling.

"So," Vik said. "You went to see your stepfather."

"No. I let myself in while they were asleep and went to his room to steal his cat. I wasn't going to hurt Bootsie, just take her home and let him worry about what had happened to her. Old Bootsie is twelve years old. He had her from the time she was a kitten. She was the only living thing in the house that he cared about." She smiled again. "I used to think he cared about Terri. Poor Terri. None of us ever understood." She dabbed at her eyes. "I wanted him to know how Momma felt. I would have brought Bootsie back sooner or later."

Marti believed that much.

"And?" Vik prompted.

"He was dead. His body was still flaccid. I didn't look at his hands and feet, but there was no rigor in his face. I checked my watch. It was 2:58. I didn't touch him. His head was just the way you found it when you got there." She took a deep breath. "At first I thought Momma might have been angry enough to do it. She was real upset about her hats. But she wouldn't have sneaked up on him in the middle of the night. He would have known what she was about to do."

"What can you tell us about the times your stepfather went to the hospital?"

"I don't know. I thought he had heart trouble, cancer. That's what Momma said. I don't know why he kept getting sick." She smiled. "Funny what guilt does. I wanted him dead for so long, thought of ways to kill him from the time I was a kid. When I found him, it was almost as if I had caused it, as if wishing had finally made it so."

"What was it like for your mother?" Vik asked. "Living with him."

"She never said. If it were me, it would have been hell. If I brought Mother something I'd make sure I had tobacco for him, one of those special blends from a tobacconist, not just something in a can."

"Why?" Vik asked.

"Because I hoped he would not . . . intrude too much because I had done something to make Mother happy. I hoped it would pacify him, that he could allow her some small pleasure without spoiling it, but I'm sure he didn't."

"He would get angry with her because you brought her . . . what?" Vik asked.

"It didn't matter. She has very dry skin. I'd bring her these Avon products that she liked or maybe pick up some lotion at Carsons."

"What would he do?"

She smiled. It wobbled into a sneer. "Clever man," she said. "He knew everybody's weak points, sore spots. By the time I walked out the door he would have thought of something. Momma would be waiting for it. By the time I was ready to go her shoulders would be hunched together as if she was going to be hit. She has arthritis in her neck and spine. I wouldn't be surprised if it got better now."

"Was he abusive?" Vik said.

Denise hesitated, then gave Vik a rueful smile. "Verbally, for so long it seemed normal." She stared into the cup. "Nothing much physically. He used to take the heel of his hand and slam it into her back. I grabbed his arm once, never saw him do it again. Toward the end, he had started spitting on her. That really upset her, the spitting."

"How long was he abusive?"

"For as long as I can remember."

"What was happening between them when he died?" Vik asked.

"He was sickly. His joints ached. He had those tumors."

"Do you think she wanted him dead?"

"No."

"Why not?"

"Finances. Her income will be much less without him. I haven't gone over it with her yet, but I'll have to help her financially. If someone treated you like he treated her for thirty-five years, having them sick, helpless, and dependent would provide a hell of a lot more satisfaction than seeing them dead."

Vik and Marti exchanged looks.

"How did you feel about that?"

"I would have enjoyed watching. In fact . . ."

Vik waited.

"When I went over there last Sunday I brought her some lotion and this candy she likes and I brought his tobacco. Hickory, his favorite. Mother took the lotion, and she looked at him, and he looked away. He had never done that before. Mother began rubbing that lotion on her arms right in front of him. She had never done that before. She'd always put whatever I brought out of his sight as quickly as possible. Watching her, I felt like cheering."

"Sounds like things had begun to change." Vik said.

"It's almost too bad that he died," Denise said. "I would have enjoyed watching her get even."

Vik made a small flicking motion with his finger. Marti nodded. There was no comeback for that statement. At least not today.

Denise began tying her scarf. "I don't know

who killed him, or why. But I know that my mother didn't do it. Not with things the way they were between them. Mother was finally getting even. I think she's relieved now that it's over, but I'm sure that she feels cheated too."

"Is there any reason why your mother would think you did it?"

"She would have heard me let myself in. She might have even got out of bed and seen me. She's not a heavy sleeper."

"Would she tell us you were there?"

Denise considered that. "Momma's lived with a lot of abuse. Not just him, but her mother, too. I've tried to make up for that, but there wasn't much I could do, just small kindnesses that brought some satisfaction to her even though he objected. She is fragile. Even though I don't think you agree. Emotionally fragile. Right now I think she's very frightened. And I think she would do just about anything if she thought she might be accused of his death." Denise looked down at her hands. "You have to understand where she's been, what she's lived through. She is not the person she would have been with a different mother, or a different husband, a different life."

Denise hesitated. "I couldn't do my job if I couldn't remember that the abused becomes the abuser, that those involved lose themselves. If it came to it, I'd confess before I'd let her spend five minutes in jail. Momma can't cope with much more. She really can't. There are so many things we need to talk about, her and I, but there's no way she can deal with it, not now."

After Denise left, Marti sat watching tiny snowflakes drift by the window. So much pain, caused by one man. There would be no justice in arresting Denise or Gladys.

"Some days you just can't win," Vik said. "Let's take all of this to Lieutenant Dirkowitz on Monday if we haven't nailed Danzel by then. I'm sure there are considerations that can be made, something that can be done."

C H A P T E R
35

Terri sat on the floor in the corner, hugging Zaar's doll. It was almost morning. She would have to hide soon. She couldn't lock the door to her bedroom. Ezra was asleep down the hall, near his mother, near Zaar. She had to go past their rooms to get downstairs. Where could she go?

She hugged the doll tighter. They weren't going to take this baby from her. She had been spotting since this morning. Not much, though, just a little bit. The other times she had told them, let them take her to the hospital, and they had taken the baby from her. This time she would not. The bleeding would stop. Everything would go away. She would keep her baby this time.

Daddy would be so proud of her. She would give him a son. He'd like little boys. He wouldn't hurt them. He wouldn't love them the way he loved her. He wouldn't want this baby to come to him.

She smiled. She had seen Daddy in church, watching Vera's little girl, Tiffany. He had asked her how old Tiffany was. Four and a half, she had told him. He had patted Tiffany's head and Tiffany had run to Vera, crying. Daddy had just smiled. That was when he decided to stop seeing the faith healer and go to a doctor. He wanted to be well enough for Tiffany. And then Zaar. She giggled. Now he was dead. Now there would never be anyone else for him but her.

She felt the warmth leaving her body, felt her nightgown and the floor getting wet, and hugged the doll closer. Little Henry would not leave her. He would never love anyone but her.

"Hush, hush, little Henry. Momma's right here. Nobody's going to take you from me. Wait until Daddy sees what a big, beautiful boy you are."

When Zaar was born, Daddy always insisted on holding her. He had fed her and changed her, he even hummed while he rocked her. Daddy had never sung to Terri. He never even talked to her when she went to him. But he talked to and sang songs to Zaar.

"Daddy's girl," he would say.

"Granddaddy," Terri would remind him. She was Daddy's girl. Still he would say, "Daddy's girl." When he tried to give Zaar back, she wouldn't take her, letting Momma or Ezra hold her instead.

"Daddy's boy," she whispered. "Daddy's boy. I'm Daddy's girl. He won't love you the way he loves me, but he'll love you, I promise he will."

The pain began, just little twinges. It was okay. The baby couldn't leave her now. She hummed the song Daddy had hummed to Zaar. She didn't know the words, but she would never forget the melody. Zaar's song, she called it, but she hummed it because it was the only lullaby she knew.

When the pains became stronger she went into the closet. Maybe they would think she had left the house and wouldn't look for her here. She had to hide from them. They would take her baby away.

C H A P T E R

36

Denise didn't want to talk with Momma about what he had done, or face her own ambivalence about how much Momma knew, how much she had overlooked, how much she had denied. But now she would have to.

When she drove by the house it was three in the morning and all of the lights were on. Instead of continuing home, she pulled into the driveway and looked inside before knocking. Momma was sitting in the living room and seemed wide awake.

"Are you all right?"

Gladys shook her head.

Denise saw the bottle of wine and the full glass and tried not to look shocked. She had never seen Momma drink anything stronger than ginger ale. "Let me help you to bed."

"No." Gladys was shivering.

Denise took off her coat. "Why is it so cold in here? He's dead now. You don't have to be cold anymore. Turn the thermostat up."

She got a blanket from the hall closet. "Here. Come sit beside me on the couch." When they were settled, she asked, "What's wrong?"

Momma didn't answer. Denise was sure she wasn't drunk, but couldn't tell if she'd begun drinking.

"Is this what you do now? Keep the lights on and drink yourself to sleep?"

Denise had just come from the hospital. Terri had lost the baby, and they were going to admit her to the psych ward as soon as possible. She hadn't seen Belle sober in months. Was Momma becoming a lush? The old man was dead and they couldn't let go of him. It had to be said, now.

But how could she begin? Momma called anything from perspiration to their menstrual cycles their "personals." The area of their body from their thighs to their navel was their "pocketbook," which was meant to be kept closed.

"Momma," Denise began, groping for words. "He touched us. He touched all of us—me, Belle, even Terri."

Beside her, Gladys trembled but said nothing.

Denise spoke to her the way she had often spoken to clients. "Terri's in the hospital. They're going to put her in a psychiatric ward. Belle's sick, too. We're all sick, Momma. He made us all sick. And pretending that none of it happened will just make it worse. He's not going to go away until we talk about this."

Gladys stared straight ahead. Denise pulled her closer, stroked her hair. Her sisters didn't understand, but she did. Terri and Belle were put off by Momma's sternness. They didn't understand how hard it was to give love when you had never been given enough. She didn't understand, either, not for a long time, but now she hugged Momma when Momma couldn't hug her.

"All those times when I had nightmares, and you came to see what was wrong? It was him. I was dreaming of him. What he did to me. What he made me do to him. He was sick, Momma. There were other little girls, too." Tears were warm on her face. She didn't want to cry.

"Della Blake told me," Gladys said. "All these years I've made like it wasn't true. I had done something wrong again. I never could do nothing right."

"All this time, Momma, and you knew?"

"What would you have had me do?" Gladys said in a harsh whisper. " 'Time Della told me, it was over. What could I do then? Leave him? Where would I go? Would you have me be like Sarah, Vera's mother, or like Della Blake? Did you want to grow up on public aid? What did I know how to do besides keep house and take care of a family?

"Pride kept me going when Momma made me clean offices and scrub floors. Pride kept me going when Joe Nathan wouldn't have me no more. Pride kept me going when Momma said she was putting us out, and I had to marry Henry so we'd have a place to live. But pride don't feed, nor clothe, no hungry, naked babies. And you were never hungry. You never wore hand-me-down clothes. Besides, 'time I found out what he had done, I was mostly out of pride by then."

Denise held her, and they cried. She wanted to ask, Why didn't you leave anyway? Why didn't you go to the police or even the reverend? But Momma did still have some pride. Too much to allow herself to believe Della. Too much to admit she had made another mistake.

37

Vik was waiting in the parking lot when Marti arrived at work Thursday morning. Sleet stung her face as she walked over to his car. It was 6:20. Lieutenant Videlko had called late last night. He wanted to see them before roll call.

"You don't think this has anything to do with killing that warrant?" she asked.

"No. Nobody in their right mind would have requested one in the first place. Sikich probably initiated this to cover his butt. He wanted an arrest and he didn't get it. He'll either complain about us or come up with some exaggerated account of everything he did to try to help break the case."

"That won't take more than a minute," Marti said. "He didn't do a damned thing but sit by his two telephones and pester us."

"Oh, he'll come up with something. People

like him always do. Too bad I can't prove he called the *News-Times*."

Lieutenant Videlko was in charge of field operations and public affairs. He worked on the first floor near the section of the precinct where civilians came to pay traffic tickets. When they entered that end of the building everything was dark. The clerks hadn't come in yet. Dim security lights flickered as they walked down the hall.

Videlko was well liked by almost everyone. Marti was certain she would have enjoyed the opportunity to work with him. He was several years older than she was, and a few inches taller than Vik. His hair was graying at the temples and he wore wire-rimmed glasses. He'd been with the department nineteen years and was on call for potential suicide or hostage situations, which, although infrequent in Lincoln Prairie, required unique talents to resolve.

As they walked into his office Videlko motioned toward two chairs.

"I gave Sikich the day off," he said, without preamble. "He'll be back with Admin and Procurement tomorrow."

Vik plunged right in. "What about his command post?"

"His what?"

"Command post, sir." Vik said. "He set one up right away in the cubicle Traffic had been using right across from our office, put in two direct lines."

"A command post?" Videlko repeated, shaking his head. "Well, he does an excellent job in Procurement, except for that toilet paper foul-up in September."

"You feeling okay, sir?" Marti asked. He looked a little pale.

"No. I feel like hell. And I'm out of here as soon as you brief me." Videlko smiled. "I don't need to see any reports. Just fill me in."

Marti smiled back. She liked being treated like a competent professional again.

After they brought Videlko up to date on the Hamilton case and the rest of their caseload, they returned to their office. The young female officer in Traffic had reclaimed her space. Marti could hear her humming. Everything was back to normal. It was almost as if Sikich had never been there.

C H A P T E R
38

By late Thursday morning, Marti was questioning Danzel Whittaker about the death of Henry Hamilton. As soon as Danzel gave Marti a sensual, inviting smile, she signaled Vik that she would interrogate. Ezra had called around nine that morning. Terri had been taken to the hospital, and Danzel, apparently fearful that he would not be able to get his hands on any of the insurance money, had gone to Ezra for his share.

"I'm here in the house alone with a killer," Ezra had whispered. "What do I do?"

"Where are you?" she asked.

"In the closet in my room where he can't hear me. But there's no lock on my door."

"Just stay there," Marti advised. "Hold on to the phone and don't make any noise. I'll send someone right over."

She had let Danzel sit in a holding cell for

over an hour. Now she and Vik were sitting across from him at the round table in the interrogation room, listening as he protested his innocence. Vik advised him that he might want an attorney present. He declined.

"We just need to talk about this, Officer," he said, speaking to Marti. "I just need to explain. This is just a misunderstanding, that's all. I haven't done anything wrong."

Danzel gave her a lopsided smile that she was sure had melted the hearts of more than a few women. "I haven't done anything wrong, honest." He smiled again. "Well, maybe, but nothing illegal."

"Sure you have," she reminded him. "You ran a confidence game. That's how we got a make on the prints you left at the Hamilton residence."

"But that was a long time ago, Officer. I was still a kid then." He tried a woebegone expression this time. "I like Terri, a lot. She's got a lot of problems. And there was nobody else in that house she could talk to. They treat her like she's five years old."

He folded his hands on the table and leaned forward. "Ezra's got more money than he can count, and he made Old Lady Hamilton help pay for the funeral. He'd never let Terri keep any of her policy. She gets an allowance. She doesn't even have a credit card or a checkbook, just what little money he feels like handing out. I just thought I could get some of the money back, for Terri. And her mother."

Danzel seemed accustomed to talking his way out of things. He seemed to expect Marti to believe this, or at least to be taken in by his boyish charm.

"Where did you say you were the night Hamilton died?"

She wrote down the address of the woman he named as an alibi.

"And when was the last time you went to his home?"

"Two days before he died."

Based on the condition of the prints and the surface where they were found, he might not be lying.

"What is your relationship with Terri Hamilton Whittaker?"

"We're just friends," he said. Then he gave her a naughty smile and shrugged. "She was really all alone in that place. The old lady was mean to her when Ezra wasn't around. And Ezra, well, he is an old man. Too old for a fine young girl like Terri."

And boys will be boys, Marti thought. "Were you the father of the baby she lost?"

He looked down at his hands. If his skin were a little lighter, Marti thought she might detect a blush. "You're both young," she said softly.

He nodded. "We were going to get our own place after the baby was born."

"And use the insurance money?"

"Just to get started. I was going to go into business for myself."

"Doing what?"

"I was going to open a record shop."

"That sounds like a wise investment. I bet you have quite a head for business."

Danzel reached out and touched her hand. "I knew you'd understand."

"Why did you go to the Hamilton house?"

"Just to check things out, help the old man. The window was stuck and he was real upset because he couldn't get it open."

"And you didn't go there Friday night? When did Hamilton find out about you and Terri?"

He stared at her and leaned back in the chair, arms folded.

"What did you tell Ezra when you asked for the money?"

"I'm not saying anything else to you," Danzel said sullenly. "Can I leave now? I've got work to do for Ezra."

Marti smiled and checked her watch. "We're going to hold you for another twenty-one hours."

"What! But I've never been in jail in my life. You can't. I mean, I haven't done anything. This isn't fair. That damned Ezra, starting this. You haven't got anyone else to blame so now you're going to pick on me. I want a lawyer. Now."

Still smiling, Marti said, "Nice talking with you."

As they walked back to their office, Vik said. "Well, he's certainly strong enough to have done it. And he could have left those prints the night Hamilton died. I'm sure his alibi will hold up initially, but if it comes down to putting the lady on the stand, it might not."

"I'd like it to be him," Marti admitted. "He thinks he's slicker than snot."

"We don't have to decide whether to charge him until tomorrow."

"He might even confess. We need to go through what we've got again. See if we can place him there at the right time."

"He drives the wrong color car," Vik said. "It's bright red. And the license plate number is nothing like Denise's. I've tried to get in touch with the guy who saw someone walking a dog, but he's never around."

"We're going to have to talk with Gladys," Marti said. "Let's get Denise on the phone and explain what's going on. Maybe she can get Gladys to cooperate."

C H A P T E R
39

Intermittent snow flurries had stopped again when Marti and Vik drove over to interview Gladys Hamilton. Vik had let his friend at the *News-Times* know that they were questioning Danzel Whittaker, and they waited until they thought Gladys would have time to read the story. If she was withholding crucial information, or had killed Henry, there was a chance that she would feel guilty about someone else being accused. Then again, she might feel relieved. Either situation could work to their advantage.

Denise met Marti and Vik at the door and they followed her to the kitchen. Marti was shocked by Gladys's appearance. Gladys was still in her bathrobe. Her hair hadn't been combed and she had dark circles under her eyes. She slumped in her chair with her elbow on the table and her forehead resting on the palm of her hand. The

News-Times on the counter had been opened and refolded. The single-paragraph article about Danzel was on the first page. Marti hoped Gladys had seen it.

Vik had decided on the way over that he would question her first. He didn't like interviews, but he had the patience and persistence it took to be a good interrogator. They thought Gladys would be cooperative, but if not, their good cop-bad cop routine worked best when Marti played bad cop. It seemed to take people by surprise.

Denise offered them seats, and Vik chose a chair at the table. Marti sat near the window, out of Gladys's line of vision.

"Momma's going to tell you everything that happened," Denise said firmly. She went to Gladys's side and patted her shoulder. "Go ahead, Momma. Tell them about Danzel first."

"I don't know what that boy told you, but Henry didn't like him and didn't want his help," Gladys said, her voice a monotone. "I'd be surprised if he even let him in the house."

"Why didn't you tell us that?" Vik asked.

"I didn't know what to tell you. I didn't know why you were asking."

"What was it that you didn't want to tell us?"

"Denise couldn't ever harm anybody."

"We know Denise was here that night," Vik said. "Can you remember anything else? Please try. It's very important."

"I didn't hear anyone else come in here. Something woke me up at least an hour and a half before Denise came. I don't know what. Something I heard while I was still sleeping." She thought for a few minutes. "A whimper, or a whining noise. I was dreaming it was Terri with her baby when I woke up. The house was quiet and I dozed off again, then Denise let herself in. I went into his room after Denise left. He was dead. I sat in the living room until daybreak. I didn't hear anything else."

Marti wondered if the sounds Gladys heard could have been made by a dog. Vik had talked with someone who had seen a man walking a dog about quarter to two. Walking a dog would have given an observer the impression that he belonged here.

"Tell them about the pokeweed," Denise prompted.

Gladys rubbed the back of her hand. "Henry didn't have heart trouble," she said, her voice just above a whisper. Marti had to lean forward to hear her.

"Wasn't nothing wrong with Henry 'til I started giving him pokeweed with his greens."

"How'd you manage that?" Vik asked.

"Just kept them in separate freezer bags and warmed them up in a little pot while I was cooking. He wouldn't come to the table until I had fixed his plate." She smiled, but there was no

mirth or joy in it. "Wasn't hard at all. My pokeweed got cooked twice like it was supposed to.
His didn't."

She sat quietly, rubbing her hand until Denise
knelt beside her and took her mother's hands in
her own. " 'Be all right now," she said. "It takes
time, but everything will be all right."

Looking from Marti to Vik, Denise said, "Is
there anything else you need to know?"

"What happened the Wednesday night before
he died?" Vik asked.

Gladys trembled. Her eyes brimmed with
tears. Denise hugged her. Marti got some Kleenex and pressed them into Gladys's hand. When
Gladys was calmer, she said, "He spit on me."
She averted her eyes.

Marti realized how ashamed she must feel.

"You must have been angry," Vik said. "Did
anyone see it happen?"

"I think Deacon Gilmore did, and maybe
Vera Holmes."

"It must have taken a lot to go to choir practice Saturday night and face all of them."

Gladys nodded.

"Why did he throw away your hats?"

"He . . . umm . . ." She hesitated. "He called
me names sometimes . . . because of . . . my
girls. I think Deacon Gilmore had words with
him after the deacons' meeting. He was angry
. . . accused me of flirting with Moses Gilmore,

of all people. While I was out . . . he threw them away . . . all of them. I'd had some of those hats for years. Three had belonged to my mother. They were gone."

Marti had one of her mother's hats. Hats were mandatory for Sunday service. Church sisters vied with each other to have the best-looking hat.

"We have something for you," Denise said. "Henry kept his papers in his army footlocker. You can break the padlock. I have no idea whether you'll find anything helpful."

When Vik lugged the olive drab trunk to their vehicle he seemed gleeful.

While Vik went through old and yellowing papers and certificates, Marti made a quick trip to the Gurnee townhouse where Danzel said his lady friend lived. A short, plump, middle-aged woman with blue eyes and blond hair opened the door and looked at Marti from the other side of a burglar chain. A Doberman pinscher greeted her with a growl.

Marti identified herself.

"If this is about Danzel, yes, he was with me the weekend before last from Friday afternoon until Sunday morning."

Marti was more interested in the dog than anything else. She didn't expect the woman to change her story at this point. A formal visit to the precinct to give a statement would give her something to think about, but that wouldn't happen unless Danzel was charged.

"Did he leave the premises for any reason?"

"Saturday afternoon, when we ran out of wine."

"Could he have left without your knowledge Friday night or early Saturday morning?"

The woman smiled and ran her tongue along her upper lip. "We weren't sleeping."

Marti drove back to the precinct in darkness. She stopped along the way for sandwiches. It might be a long night. When she reached their office Vik was drumming his fingers on some papers that were spread out on his desk.

"What have you got?" Marti asked.

"Damned if I know."

"What's it look like?"

"Don't know that either."

He helped himself to a steak sub while she scanned the items on his desk: a ledger page, three invoices for $5,000 each that were dated October 17, 1965, from A—Z Carpentry in Arlington Heights, and looked at the name handwritten on a manila envelope. "Moses Gilmore? Why does his name keep popping up? Gladys mentioned him today. He's a real gentleman."

Vik pulled the tab on a can of Mellow Yellow. "Everything else in the footlocker makes sense.

Discharge papers, wedding license, birth and death certificates for various family members, and ledgers for every penny Hamilton earned or spent for the last fifty years or damned near it. And those papers that you're looking at. They must be important, because what they were with is important, but you tell me what that means."

She told him about the Doberman.

"The guy who saw the man with the dog will be home tonight. Maybe he's remembered something else, and maybe, just maybe, it'll be of more use than what's on my desk."

They ate in silence until Vik said, "Does Gilmore have a dog?"

"I didn't see one."

"Just curious."

Marti thought about it for a few minutes and called Gladys. "He's asthmatic—allergic to dogs, cats too, and never came to their house because of Bootsie."

"Just a thought," Vik said. "The way he was hanging around her at the wake . . ."

"Was he? I saw him standing near her once, but she didn't seem to be paying much attention to him."

"That's why we both went, MacAlister. You don't have eyes in back of your head. You're right about him being a gentleman. He was waiting for her at the church hall. He helped her with her coat, got her a cold drink, suggested she eat.

Not that Gladys seemed pleased. She walked away from him every chance she got, but he was persistent."

Gilmore had talked a lot about Gladys. "Unrequited love?" Marti said.

Vik's telephone rang at 8:25. "Damn," he said when he hung up. "Just what we need, some guy wearing a long coat, that was kind of blowing in the wind, walking a German shepherd."

"Moses Gilmore," Marti said, "wears an old army greatcoat."

CHAPTER
40

Gilmore is allergic to dogs," Marti said. "I didn't see any sign of one while I was there. He said he was at the hospital Friday night."

Vik rearranged the odd assortment of papers he'd found in Hamilton's footlocker. "I think we have to talk with him," Vik said. "And give him Miranda first. I want to see if he reacts when he sees these papers. Besides, we've got to decide whether or not to charge Whittaker by morning. We can't with loose ends like this."

Reluctantly, Marti agreed.

When Moses Gilmore was brought to the precinct for questioning, he refused to speak with them until he had talked with Reverend Douglas and an attorney. Marti asked them both to come in as soon as possible.

It was 11:30 before Gilmore was ready to talk. He requested an envelope that was in his wallet.

Photographs, the sergeant said. Marti said he could have them during their interview.

Everyone met in their office as a courtesy to the reverend. A sheriff's deputy waited outside the door. The Reverend Douglas, who had been allowed to speak with Gilmore, was tight-lipped and angry. Yolanda Winfield, the attorney representing Gilmore, yawned. She was wearing slacks and a sweater and looked as if she might have been awakened to come here. Yolanda was one of three black attorneys who practiced in Lincoln Prairie, and had just passed the bar a year ago.

"Mr. Gilmore is ready to make a statement," she said.

Vik had seated Gilmore beside his desk. Now he fussed with the yellowing invoices. Deacon Gilmore seemed to know what they were.

"I suppose Henry left those papers where Gladys could find them."

"She gave them to us," Vik said.

Gilmore nodded. "Henry liked starting something and then sitting back and watching what happened next. All innocent and self-righteous he'd be, and surprised if folks went to fussing and arguing after he made some little comment or let something he'd overheard slip out."

The recording officer gave Marti a look that implied he'd prefer to hear something of importance.

"So self-righteous, an upright man before the

308

Lord." Gilmore said this the way some men would speak profanities. "And all the time, coveting that child, Vera Miles. I heard him and Gladys arguing about Vera. Gladys told him it was time he left those Holmes women alone, that he had slept with Vera's mother and that was enough."

Gladys had withheld something else from them, Marti thought. Did she really believe it was Sarah Holmes whom Henry had been involved with, or did she tell herself that so she wouldn't have to confront the truth?

"Henry knew how I felt about Gladys. That's why he took up with her in the first place. He told me so."

Gilmore asked for the envelope and took out some old black-and-white snapshots. A picnic, a church social, some formal occasion, a wedding, perhaps—women working in the kitchen and shepherding children into church. Gladys, caught unaware, never looking at the camera. Had he been carrying these photographs around all these years?

"Wild she was inside," he said. "Wild with Joe Nathan. She would have been wild with me. I would never have done her like Henry did. He took all that she was and destroyed it. He knew I loved her. He sneaked and married her while I was on vacation. Laughed at me when I got back, said I was a fool to think Gladys would ever want the likes of me. I would have been good to her. Henry treated her like dirt. He spit on her Wednesday night." Gilmore's voice rose. "He spit on her." He raised his fist. "He spit!"

Gilmore slumped in the chair, as if his anger were spent. Tears came to his eyes. "What kind of a man does that? All those years—he took everything that she was, and then he spit in her face."

Marti didn't speak or move. She was almost holding her breath.

"Henry had heart trouble, had cancer. He'd been to the hospital half a dozen times," Gilmore said. He sounded as if he was reciting something he'd practiced again and again. "With all that, I thought everyone would think he just died in his sleep."

Without raising his hand from his desk, Vik spread his fingers in a V sign, but he didn't look pleased. Marti made a V sign too. She'd have to call Denise tonight to let her know.

"It was his head, wasn't it?" Gilmore said. "I raised the pillow once, and he looked at me. If he had asked to live I couldn't have killed him. But he was so frightened. I'd seen the fear in Gladys's eyes when he was displeased, and now he was scared of me. I held that pillow on his face until he was still. That's how I will always remember him, helpless and scared and begging me with his eyes, just like I used to see Gladys beg him."

"Then you went to the hospital?" Marti asked.

"What with having my tenant's dog in the car and being in the house that had a cat, I had an asthma attack. Cat ran out when I got the door open. Scared me half to death."

Vik held up an invoice. "What about these?"

"Oh, that," Gilmore said. "Just one of Henry's little tricks. He volunteered me and Deacon Franklin to do all of our work on the church for free, without asking us first. It was okay the first time, when we built it. I didn't need the money. But when we put on the addition, Henry did it again, and that time, I did. Henry said he'd pay me under the table." He motioned to the papers. "That's how he did it.

"Then he thought he had something to hold over me. He did, in a way, but only because I didn't want Gladys to think I needed the money. My daddy used to do yard work and odd jobs for her people. I was always poor to her. I didn't want her to keep thinking of me that way."

He turned to the reverend. "I might have to get right with the Lord for all that I've done, but God knows what Henry did to Gladys and he knows I put a stop to that. Now Gladys will know, too. There's still time for us. What can they do to an old man?"

Vik called Denise. They didn't go home until all of the paperwork was completed. This was one case that Marti wanted to put behind her.

C H A P T E R
41

When Belle left the club the bartender locked up behind her. She leaned against the building to get her bearings, squinting into the darkness.

Her bus would be at the corner in five minutes and she had to pass a bunch of kids to get there. Belle tucked her bottle of scotch under her arm. She was smarter than those kids. Walking carefully so that she wouldn't stumble and fall, she crossed to the other side of the street to avoid them.

The wind blew open her coat. She should have buttoned it. If she put the bottle down . . . the bus reached the corner while she was still half a block away. Yelling, she tried to run for it. As it pulled away, she tripped and went down on one knee. The bottle smashed against the sidewalk. Scotch ran to the gutter. She could smell it. Damn.

When she tried to get up, her knee hurt. She crawled over to the curb and sat there for a minute. At least the kids weren't paying any attention to her. She didn't know when the next bus would come. She didn't have cab fare. She didn't even have anything to drink. She got up and limped toward the corner.

Hands grabbed her before she got there and pulled her into a building. Hands snatched her purse and began pulling at her clothes. Angry, she tried to get free, feeling his breath hot on her neck, smelling wine. Then she relaxed. She'd been raped before. What the hell. What would he do, rape and kill her? Old Henry had already done that. She looked at his face. Just a kid.

"Hey, daddy," she said. "What you want? No need to get it like this."

"Huh?"

She tried to put her arms around him but he pushed her hands away.

"Oh, daddy, come on. Let baby give you something good."

He opened her purse, took her wallet, and threw the purse down. "You're crazy," he said as he turned and ran. "You're crazy!"

Winded, she leaned against the wall and tried to brush away the dirt, smooth down her hair.

Damn. The West Side of Chicago, a dozen murders a day and she couldn't even get herself killed. She went into the night air again, felt the cold wind in her face, walked past the kids, who ignored her. She went to the pay phone outside of the store on the corner and called collect.

"Denise. Please come get me. Please come. Help me, Denise. Please help me."

She didn't want to get raped again. She didn't want to be dead.

CHAPTER
42

On Monday morning, Lieutenant Dirkowitz returned from his seminar but didn't send for Marti and Vik until late in the afternoon. Tall, broad-shouldered, and blond, he was standing by the window, looking toward the lake. Drizzle had given away to a gray, cloudy day. Still no sunshine. Marti was certain this was a record. Maybe tonight she'd get home early enough to watch the weather report on the evening news.

Dirkowitz offered them a seat and began toying with the defused hand grenade he kept on his desk. "I'm sorry that by some oversight on my part, Howie Sikich was third in command. I never even thought about what would happen if Videlko couldn't take over for me. Sikich is good at procurement but he's totally ineffective in dealing with people. And I'm sure he was a pain in the ass."

Marti appreciated his honesty. She had never heard an officer in his position speak this way before.

"You should not have had to conduct investigations under those conditions. I have an extremely low tolerance for incompetence." He pulled the pin on the hand grenade and made a noise like a small explosion.

"Now, I'm recommending both of you for a commendation for the way you handled the Hamilton case. It has nothing to do with Sikich, but since he didn't file a complaint for insubordination I'll give you two extra days off—if you can find the time to take them."

"Why a commendation, sir?" Vik asked.

Marti gave his ankle a discreet kick. Who cared?

"This was just a routine investigation," Vik said, ignoring her.

"And one that was totally contained within the community. It stayed there. The details didn't hit the newspapers. Reverend Douglas and I are on several committees and I would have been upset if his church received any adverse publicity. Then there's Denise Stevens. I've gone through your reports and I appreciate your thoroughness and your restraint. Denise brings a great deal of sensitivity and determination to her work and she's the most effective probation officer in the department."

He pulled the pin on the grenade again. "I'm recommending you because this is what policing is all about. Going into the community, treating its members with respect, exercising discretion and common sense. This is what we're paid to do, and frankly, if you receive recognition for this it'll send a message to the rest of the department."

He dropped the hand grenade on the desk, signaling the end of the meeting.

"See, Jessenovik," Marti said as they walked down the hall. "This is what happens when you hang out with a big city cop. Commendations."

"Hah! This is what happens when a big city cop learns how to do real police work. We reason, we think things through, we don't draw our weapons on every little pretext. . . ."

"Right, right. I don't want to hear that again. When you go to roll call with two guys in the morning and they get blown away on a routine traffic stop four hours later, you pull your weapon every time you exit your vehicle. Trust me, I know."

As the reached the stairwell Vik turned to her. "Did that really happen?"

"Yes. But only once."

When they got to their office, Marti's whole family was waiting by her desk: Theo, Joanna, Sharon, and Lisa.

"What's up?" Marti asked.

Sharon looked conservative in slacks, a jacket, and high heels, but she'd blown it a bit with turquoise beads at the end of each of her dozens of braids, and large matching earrings. "Ready to go?"

"Where?"

"A family celebration!" Theo said. "We're meeting Ben and Mike at the restaurant. We're all taking you to dinner."

"Vik, too," Joanna said. "Ben's picking up Mrs. Jessenovik."

"Is that so," Vik said, not quite managing to look stern.

"Yes," Theo grinned. "And Ma says you love sweet potato pie, so Ben's bringing two for your Thanksgiving dinner. Joanna baked them."

"And don't tell us you have to fill out any reports first," Sharon warned. "I'm going to see your lieutenant if you do. The Hamilton case is closed. Denise is okay. And we're celebrating."

Marti didn't mention the commendation. She wanted Vik to tell Mildred first.

On Friday, Marti had lunch with Denise at Al's Soul Food City, a small restaurant on Thirty-fifth Street. It was Denise's idea. The lighting was dim and the booths private. They had the special of the day: all-you-can-eat fried catfish, hush puppies, and hominy grits. It was the first time Marti had seen Denise eat a meal.

"The lieutenant told me you stopped an arrest warrant. I had no idea. Thank you."

"Thank Vik. I didn't have enough clout. But I'm glad that he did."

"I know. And I appreciate that."

"How's Belle?" Marti asked.

"She's talking to people this time, about what happened. Maybe she'll make it."

"At least she's trying."

"I know. Even if she doesn't stick it out for thirty days . . . they say if nothing else, it screws up your drinking. Well . . . we'll see."

Marti didn't ask about Terri. According to Sharon, she had been transferred to a private psychiatric hospital for long-term care. She didn't inquire about Gladys, either.

"How's Zaar?"

"She's with Momma."

"She is?"

Denise smiled, a big smile that showed her dimples. "And they're doing okay. I get over there every day, even if it's just for a few minutes, and I'm beginning to see a difference. Zaar spoke yesterday. And Momma called just before I left. She baked a cake and got Zaar to stick her finger in the bowl."

Denise munched on a hush puppy. "Sounds crazy, doesn't it? Coaxing a child to do things as ordinary as that. But Terri—" She shook her head. "I kept telling Ezra not to force the child on her, to just let his mother take care of her. I told Momma that this was her last shot at being a good mother and she'd better not blow it. She's working on getting Zaar to sit in her lap and letting us hug her."

Marti looked at her for a minute. Denise seemed as happy as she'd ever seen her. "You're a remarkable woman."

"I'm a survivor. So are you. And we are legion."

They finished their meal in a companionable silence.